Even In Eden

A.M. Glory

Published by Gloryous Publishing LLC

Harrison AR

www.gloryouspublishing.com

ISBN: 979-8-9943898-0-5

First Edition: February 2026

Printed in the United States of America A.M. Glory

DEDICATION

For all those who have felt oppressed by the written word.
May you find the ones that liberate you.

ACKNOWLEDGMENTS

To Skylar, who never let me doubt myself for long, thank
you for the unwavering hype.
To Richie, for manning the fort which allows me to escape
and write this book without returning to ruin.
And to my friends and family, who may not be the audience
for this book, for cheering all the same.

Spoiler Warning

To support informed reading, the following content notice mentions sensitive themes though may allude to elements of the story and diminish impact.

Content Warning

This book contains mature themes intended for adult readers, including but not limited to: heresy, religious trauma, sexual assault, post-traumatic stress disorder (PTSD), postpartum depression, and explorations of sexuality. Reader discretion is advised.

About the Author

A.M. Glory has always lived somewhere between story and myth. Raised on inherited legends, half-remembered truths, and a deep instinct to question what she was told, she learned early that meaning is something you uncover, not something you're handed.

Her work draws from personal lore as much as ancient myth, weaving together themes of forbidden love, autonomy, misplaced faith, and awakening. She writes for those who have felt themselves change quietly, irrevocably, and for whom desire was never a sin, but a revelation.

A.M. Glory is the founder of Gloryous Publishing LLC, an independent press devoted to bold voices and untamed stories.

PROLOGUE

In the beginning…there was silence.
Not absence, but anticipation. Like the held breath
before the first note in a symphony. Then the breath
released, gentle, yet commanding. Calling light into
existence.

That light busted free, like a sprout from the seed of
nothingness, spilling gold across the void.
Sky rose above the waters, and the waters gave
birth to the earth. Order carved itself from chaos,
trembling yet determined, and the pulse of creation
began to beat.
From that rhythm bloomed a place of soft light and
sacred stillness.

A garden.

Where the breath of creation lingered sweet and
heavy. It was the first of its kind. Unbounded by walls
or borders. It simply was, unfolding gently from the

pulse of creation.

Scent lingered heavy in the air. Myrrh, fig, and the clean musk of new earth. Air hummed with the quiet ache of potential. Leaves whispered to one another, still remembering the voice that called them into being. The rivers wound through golden reeds like veins of the divine body, carrying the blood of the sea.

Nothing had yet known sorrow. The world was expectant. Balanced. Nothing was excessive, nothing was lacking. It was *perfect*.
The ground beneath was rich and yielding, warm from the recent touch of divine hands.

Moss spread like velvet over stone. Flowers opened with urgency, their petals unfurling slowly, deliberately, as though savoring the act of becoming. Some climbed on vines upward, bold, drinking deeply from the sky. Others blooms low to the earth, shy, their fragrance mingling with the soil.

And from the soil, God formed **Man**.

Not in thunder or flame, but with the patient pressure of divine fingers kneading earth. Clay became flesh. Breath became will. Limbs strong and steady, eyes unclouded and curious, the first spark of thought flickered there.
God named him **Adam**, and the name settled on the wind like a decree.

He rose, unsteady but whole, and began to name the world as if words could contain its wonder. *Lion,* he said, and the creature bowed its head. *River,* and water curved obediently toward his feet. With each name, something of power passed from heaven to tongue, until the garden itself waited for his next utterance.

But what of the first woman?

Not the one shaped from Adam's bone or borrowed breath. No shadow, no echo, no second draft. The one who stood beside him at the moment of dawn, carved from the same red earth, under the same sun.

Time tried to forget her.
Man tried to rewrite her.
But before there was legend, there was **Lilith**.

Where Adam was given dominion, she was given curiosity and ambition.
When he named, she listened, not to memorize, but to understand the way sound shaped into living decree. And when she spoke her own name, the garden itself stilled, as though hearing the language of its making.

Lilith.

The syllables thrummed through soil and sky. A new kind of power awoke. Not the power to label what was, but what could be. Vines curled around her ankles, recognizing their mother. The reeds swayed toward her voice. Creation bent, not in submission, but in resonance.

Adam watched. At first in wonder, then in unease. There was something in her gaze, that quiet challenge of a mirror that reflects too truly. She looked at him, curious, assessing, the corners of her mouth curved as if she already knew a secret he did not.

When she turned her eyes upward to the unclaimed expanse above, he spoke quickly, eager to define and cement his place.

"*Heaven*," he said, proud of the certainty in his own voice. He would name ALL things, sure his knowledge not be questioned, as it had been bestowed by God himself.

Her gaze snapped back to him. Then she inclined her head, slow and measured, the way one humors a child. She turned her eyes to the sky again and into the large expanse before her. Her eyes were new, and so was her mind. It was an abyss, bottomless and with each passing second seeking to be filled with knowledge. Knowledge of her existence, and the things that surrounded her. She didn't want to know their names as much as she wanted to understand why they were what they were. Why the trees stood stall, yet bowed to the waters below? Why the creatures around them looked so different? She wanted to know their thoughts, to know if their appearance was their sole difference.

One of the *Lions*, as Adam named, approached her with reverence. On reaching her feet, it crouched. She mirrored, falling to one knee. Trailing her hand through it's mane, until she reached it's chest, and the heartbeat within. She froze. Instantly, she knew there was more to it than just the name. She brought her other hand to her own breast, and felt the same beat in it, though an entirely different rhythm. Then placing that same hand on the soil beneath her feet. Though faint, he felt the same thrumming.

"*Soul*." She whispered in understanding. "The seat of all thoughts and dwelling of the spirit."

"It is a lion, as I have said." Adam declared, reducing the entire existence of the majestic creature to just a name. "You are feeling the beat of a heart." He attempted to correct, and missing the point entirely.

"That is the first animal I named. There are many more, the cattle, the wolves, the birds. I can teach you their names." He offered proudly.

He straightened his back and raised his head, as if to convey he was worth much more than what currently occupied her attention. Lilith regarded him closely, not entirely interested in names. She was interested in what was yet to be named, and the soul of the man who didn't know he had one.

They were made to be companions, co-creators of paradise. But balance is a fragile thing when one hand believes itself the weightier.

Adam's days became full of words: commands to the beasts, proclamations to the sky. Lilith's became full of watching, the subtle arrogance in his stance, the way his naming left no room for listening. It was almost as if he felt he needed no help, and knew all there was to know. With each passing day he re-lived the same events, as if it was his sole purpose. As if he had no alternatives. Lilith had limited patience for it.

Still, she lingered near him, half-fascinated. His strength was crude, untested; his faith in his own rightness burned almost beautifully. Sometimes, when he laughed, the sound reminded her of the first crack of light. But pride began to sour that music.

One night came like all the others before. The moon spilled silver through the canopy, softening the edges of the world. They lay upon moss that still smelled of the divine hand that shaped it. The air was warm, alive with the hush of unseen wings.

"You must lie beneath me," Adam said, "and be filled with me."
He said it as if repeating a truth already written.

Lilith's eyes narrowed. The stars burned in them like coals.
"I do not belong to you," she answered, voice eerily calm as still water. "Nor *beneath* you."

He frowned, uncertain of how to face this rejection. "It is the order of things," he insisted. "I was given dominion over all things created. I say it as it should be, as it was made to be."

Her smile was slight, pitying. "We were shaped of the same earth. I will not pretend it bows differently for you."

Adam's throat grew dry, a mix of desire, anger, and fear. But of all the emotions that took hold of him, one stood at the helm and it was determination.

She dared challenge the order that God himself had set? That in itself was an abomination.

The clash of her defiance was not loud, yet it filled the garden. The trees shivered. The beasts turned their heads. Even the river seemed to pause in its song.

He rose and sought the comfort of command. "You will submit," he said, voice louder now, as if to drown the doubt coiling in his chest.

Lilith just stared back, rage in her eyes.

Her silence aggravated him further. As if to say he

wasn't even worthy of a reply.

Adam, unaccustomed to disobedience, spoke to God. "*She defies her role*," he said loudly and with gravity in his voice. "She questions the order!"

But God did not answer.

The sky gave no thunderous approval.
Only silence, a vast, knowing silence.

Lilith laughed then, low and rich, taking pleasure in Adam's posturing being met the silence she felt it deserved. The sound of her laughter slithered through the garden like smoke. It coiled around Adam, and left him shivering.

That night he *lay alone*, his dreams haunted by the echo of her taunting laughter, a sound he promised himself he would never hear again.

When dawn came, she was gone.

He searched the garden, calling her name, but the trees whispered back in tongues he could not understand. When he tired, he assumed she had been *unmade*. That God had corrected the error that was her creation. He took it as validation of his place in Eden. And in his relief, **he forgot**.

But she not unmade, she was not cast out, and she did not run. She *walked away*.

Barefoot, bare-skinned, into the parts of Eden where no paths existed and nothing yet had names. With each step that carried her farther from "*Adam's Dominion*", she felt power expand.

Although she couldn't yet put a finger on it. She knew something out there beckoned to her, fulfillment and perhaps a truth Eden had yet to reveal

At the garden's edge, creation grew uncertain. The soil trembled, unsure whether to exist. She inhaled; the smell of wet soil made her smile. That smile stretched, as did her mind, creating room for endless possibilities of what *could be*.

She knelt, pressed her palms into the raw earth, and breathed. From that breath, a new garden grew, one not spoken into being by decree, but coaxed forth by desire.

She closed her eyes and summoned new creatures. Some purred, some hissed, *none bowed*. Among them, the serpents slithered close, their tongues tasting the new power that thrummed in the air. They whispered in secret languages, and Lilith smiled. For she understood them all, and they understood her.

Here was no obedience, no hierarchy, no command.

Here was instinct made holy.

And when she spoke again, her voice wove through leaf and flame and flesh alike. *This* was creation unbridled, not the naming of what already was given, but of what she thought to give. She named it all into being.

She became the mother of creation, of nature. Not ruler, not lord, just kin.

Lilith's garden did not rival Eden; it expanded it. It did not forbid knowledge; it rewarded hunger for it.

Her garden was not forbidden, just hidden. And no man ever found it.

Of course, this was never really a *man's* story.

CHAPTER

ONE

For **Eve**, Eden was everything.

The rivers shimmered like veins of light through living soil, winding toward some unseen heart. Trees stood in perfect poise, strong and peaceful, as their roots whispered together beneath her feet. Fruit hung heavy, ready and waiting; its perfume sweet enough to make the air taste of it. Even the wind sang softly through the reeds, carrying a tune that seemed to know her name.

Eve cherished it all. She adored the sound of leaves gossiping above her head, the glimmer of fish darting in clear pools, the way every color felt truer than sight alone could hold. The garden was alive, and she could feel its pulse through her bare soles as she walked.

And Adam made everything make sense. He had been the very first thing her eyes beheld. Her beginning and likely her ending. His presence calmed her and made her feel cherished.

And Eve was grateful.

Morning in Eden did not arrive so much as unfold, petal-soft, sun warmed, drifting in like a breath held by the world and slowly released.

Eve stepped barefoot into the meadow just as the mist lifted. Dew jeweled the wildflowers in glistening beads, catching the light like tiny, trapped suns. Golden cone flowers swayed beside feathery lavender blooms; their stems cool against her palms as she waded through them. Every color here seemed to hum. Yellow warming into amber. Violet fading into soft pink. Green so deep it felt like the memory of water.

Behind her, Adam stirred awake beneath the sheltering willow. Its long green curtains trailed down in soft whispers, stirring with the wind, casting lacework shadows over the mirrored pool below. The branches draped like the creator's arms, gentle and protective, though Eve had never heard the tree speak in anything but the language of leaves. She sometimes wondered how it felt. Reaching toward the water with its many hanging branches, was it just content growing where it stood, or was it desperately reaching for more moisture than was given.

"Eve?" Adam called sleepily; the sound thick with a day's voice not yet spoken. "You rise before the sun."

She smiled at him over her shoulder. "It's on its way, I thought I'd greet it."

He groaned, pushing himself off the earth. Grains of

soil sticking to his side, as if seeking comfort. He dusted it off.

"I wish I knew why this fascinates you so."

Eve's lips curled in a smile. Something about this world they shared always delighted her, but even she couldn't define it. But she remained unbothered by the logic behind her joy. The feeling was enough for her.

She felt his warmth behind her, then she felt his strong arms curl around her waist from behind. Together they watched the sun peak out from the horizon, just before generously bathing the garden in it's warmth.

Soon the chirping and whistling of birds filled the air, as they skimmed low over the water, catching gnats in glittering wakes. The surface rippled in rings, each one catching a shard of sunlight in fragments.

Adam kissed the top of her head, lingering a moment. "Another beautiful day in paradise, but you, make it perfect."

A faint smile touched her lips, and she drew his hand up, kissing the open palm. She could feel unbridled strength pulse through his hands. Strength that could break anything half. Yet, she had only ever known those hands to be gentle.

But Eve didn't always feel perfection the way he did. Beauty, yes. Wonder, endlessly. But there was an emptiness in her chest sometimes, a strange ache beneath her ribs, as if the world was a puzzle and she'd been given only most of the pieces.

She turned to look up into Adam's adoring eyes, searching for any sign of the same restlessness she felt swirling inside. Something that told her she was not alone, or peculiar for feeling this way.

"Do you ever feel…Incomplete? Like there is something missing." She asked. His gaze thinned, and she sighed. "I don't know how to explain it."

"Oh, I do understand. I once felt that way, lonely. Then I prayed to God for a companion that saw me for what I truly was. He made you from my ribs, to complete me. To be my mate."

 Eve's face dropped only slightly before she caught herself. He didn't really understand her restless mind. He seemed steady and sure. For him there was only one thing more perfect than Eden, and that was her.

She at least could take solace in knowing her purpose so easily. She tucked the thoughts away in the dark recesses of her mind, unsure if her questions even had answers. Perhaps there was something wrong with her. Maybe these thoughts were akin to questioning God's plan for her. She didn't want that, she wanted nothing more than to be what she was *Meant to be.*

Eve pressed a kiss to his lips, feeling their softness. He groaned, tightening his grip on her waist. She could already feel his manhood twitch, but it was too early to indulge in his urges.

"Perhaps we could continue this later," she suggested softly, trying to step out of his arms. But against his firm hold, her effort was wasted.

"I need you now." He said in a husky voice.

"And you'll always have me." She planted another kiss on his lips. "We've only just risen, we have the rest of the day to fulfill your needs." She assured lightly.

Finally, he loosened his grip and she took her leave in favor of her daily search. The forage for fruit, roots, nuts, and other sustenance the garden would provide today. But also in search of something to quench the thirst she felt.

She moved through Eden with open palms and wide eyes, her steps unhurried, her breath in rhythm with the wind. She knew the name of every creature and bird. As it was Adam's duty to name them, it was hers to listen and remember, to tend, to nurture. The lion would lower its massive head to her touch, the doe would rest its chin against her knee. She fed them from her hand and spoke softly to them in earnest, and they seemed to understand her intention, if not her words.

A thin silver stream veined through the forest before feeding into the larger stronger river. Eve followed it, bare feet soundless in the moss that clung to the stones. The air was a calming cool here, shadowed by towering trees whose leaves glowed like stained glass when the sun began its climb. Rays of light filtered through in luminous gold columns, illuminating drifting pollen like suspended stars.

A young deer drank from the stream, unafraid as she approached. Its flank glittered with droplets, white spots gleaming in the early light. When it raised its head, its eyes regarded her with quiet recognition, as though it had been expecting her.

This happened often.

Animals did not fear them. They stepped toward her, not back. They bowed their heads or brushed their flanks along her legs, communicating without words.

Today, the deer nudged her palm with its soft nose.

She always suspected they had plenty to say.

Past the stream, the forest opened into one of Eden's many meadows, this one an open sea of wildflowers swaying in waves of gold, rust, and pale pink. The petals brushed her calves, warm from sun, cool at their bases where dew still clung. A breeze swept through, rolling the field like a soft sigh.

Far off, she could now see Adam collecting olives from the grove. Later she would smash them to remove their skin, and cure them in water.

He was strong, purposeful, carving paths by patience alone. Eden adored him because he did the work of cultivating: gathering, carrying, naming, building. But Eden responded to Eve.

Eve stood for a moment, regarding Adam while he worked. He moved with the easy strength of someone shaped by the earth itself, broad chest rising steadily, muscles shifting beneath dark sun-warmed skin. His black curls clung to his temples in a subtle sweat, framing eyes, green as picked sage beginning to wilt. The lines of his face were sharp yet softened by the warmth he carried in his expression; a straight nose, full mouth, and a jaw dusted with dark beard that made him look older than he felt. His skin carried the scent of sun, fig leaves, and the salt of honest joyful work. Even in stillness, Adam felt like motion waiting to happen. Tension in his shoulders, hands always half-curled as though ready to build or to name or to hold. His gaze was steady, almost earnest, and when he looked at her it was with the uncomplicated devotion of someone without doubts.

Eve was drawn to that certainty in him, as she began to close the distance. The deer following close behind.

"They like you more than me," Adam joked as he noticed her approaching.

"Only because I eat slower," she teased, plucking one of the olives from his hand and offering it to their young friend.

He grinned, brushing a strand of her hair behind her ear. "I think they see you as I do."

They walked together through the meadows, bees humming lazily around them. Beyond the tree line, the landscape shifted, rolling into lush forest again, deeper and thicker. When the path forked, Adam veered left toward the place he preferred: the sun, open air, the wide simplicity of the world.

Eve hesitated, glancing toward the path to the right.

That path was different.

The vines grew thicker there, draping from branches like curtains. The air felt cooler, charged, almost sacred. The forest whispered more urgently along that way. She felt tugged by it, like a memory without an owner.

Adam noticed her pause.

"You always look down that path," he said playfully. "As if you find the obstacles of complicated terrain enticing."

"Do you not hear it?" she asked, genuinely curious.

He laughed softly. "Trees creak, reeds rustle, the same water runs. That is all."

But Eve heard something else. A murmur beneath the surface of sound. Like a name she had never been given.

She would not follow it today.

Adam intertwined their fingers, and she let him lead her down the well-worn path where shafts of sunlight turned the air golden and warm. Butterflies rose in colorful clouds as they flew across flowers.

They came upon the lion resting beneath an ancient tree, his mane the color of ripe wheat. His paw lay gently across the back of a lamb that slept contentedly beside him. The lion lifted his head when Eve approached, regarding her with warm amber eyes.

"Peace to you," Eve whispered, running her fingers through his mane.

He rumbled softly, leaning into her touch.

Adam looked on with fond pride. "Even the great kings of the wild adore you."

"They adore the world," she said. "As do I."

The lamb bleated softly, brushing its nose against Eve's hand before curling back against the lion.

Later, when Adam went to tend the distant grape terraces, Eve wandered again toward the water.

A turtle basking on a sun-warm rock, small claws gripping slick moss. When Eve sat beside the stream, the turtle turned its wise, wrinkled face toward her. A moment passed between them, still, reverent.

It blinked slowly. And she smiled.

Further upstream, through the trees, she saw the apes perched on branches, studying her. Not frightened, curious. Always curious. They climbed from branch to branch, occasionally stopping to talk amongst themselves in sounds that weren't hers to know.

Eve remained by the water, unsettled, but not afraid. The forest around her boasted with life: the hum of insects, the call of birds.

She lifted her gaze toward the deeper forest. The right-hand path still waited, shrouded in shadowed green, blanketed in pale fog, vines swaying gently as though to veil a secret.

One day, she thought, *she would follow it*.

One day, she would learn all Eden had to offer.

TWO

When she slept, she dreamed only of colors or warmth, as what more could a sleeping mind want that it wouldn't find in waking hours. When she woke, she could find no reason to want for anything at all. No reason to wander any further.

And yet, she did.

She often found herself wanting something she couldn't name. Something a part of her mind told her existed but was just beyond her reach.

There was no word for what she felt. If there had been, she might have feared it more.

Instead, she simply wandered, in search of it. Nearly each morning, rising with the first light, the dew still trembling on the grass like diamonds shaken loose from the stars. A small bird's song carried above her, a melody so perfect it seemed impossible for one throat to hold.

This morning, went to the spring she loved best, a pool lined with rose quartz and soft grass. At the base of the large willows that also sheltered them in slumber. The water was clear as the dragonfly's wing, cool at its depths and warm where the sun reached it. She waded in, sighing softly as it closed around her. The temperature was perfect and made her moan in satisfaction. She shut her eyes, and let her worries dissolve in the water.

When she rose from the spring, water slid down her copper skin like a blessing. The sunlight kissed her shoulders.

Eve's beauty had a warmth to it, gentle and inviting. Her hair fell around her shoulders in wild curls, the color of dark honey but lighter at the ends where the sun had kissed them. Her hazel eyes shifted with the light, sometimes green, sometimes gold, always bright with wonder. Her skin glowed, smooth and soft, giving her a golden glow that made even the shadows seem gentler around her. There was a natural grace in the way she moved, unselfconscious and fluid. Her lips were full, often curving upward in small, thoughtful smiles. The line of her jaw was delicate. The curves of her body soft and full. The air itself seemed to embrace her, curling around her like the breath of a paramour.

Like Adam.

He was good.
Strong and sure, steady in his kindness. He could tell the difference between every leaf, every feather, every

grain of soil. He loved her as one might love the first fire lit; reverently, proudly, certain it had been made for him.

When she first awoke to this world, she had seen only his face, those eyes filled with wonder, with relief so pure it had nearly broken her new heart. He told her she was the answer to his prayers. That for many years, he had asked to not be alone anymore. God had answered him.

She was his answer.

She listened as he spoke of the world, of what had come before. How he had been given the charge of naming, how the world had been empty of voice until he spoke. He told her of the lion and the dove, of the sun and moon, of the God that created them and the Devil that defied God and was cast out.

She listened, and she remembered all the things he had told her. She learned the words he loved, and in learning them, she learned him.

He had taught her to speak of the world as it was, and she found beauty in repetition. When he smiled at her across a field of poppies or pulled her close beneath the olive trees, there was warmth, and peace, and something like safety.

She shaped herself around that peace, careful and content.

He was her world and she knew him well. Like the way he parted his lips, just before he answered her barrage of questions. The way he smiled when she kissed him and his chest drummed an irregular beat.

She understood every twitch of his eyes and curl of his lips. It was her duty, for how could she meet his needs, without knowledge of him.

Eve tended a small garden of her own beyond the citrus grove, a patch of herbs and flowering vines in a perfect circle of soil. It required little; nothing in Eden ever demanded much before it offered reward. But she reveled in the feel of the earth between her fingers, pressing her hands into the pulse of creation. Sometimes she would hum softly as she worked, brushing pollen from her knees, tasting berries still warm from the sun.

Adam often found her there, and his face would brighten. Sometimes she got the feeling that he hadn't simply happened upon her by chance, the way he pretended to. There was a part of him that was protective and worried she might vanish.

"You make the world more beautiful," he'd praise her. "You were made for this."

She would smile, and mean it.

It meant so much to have someone who believed in her and constantly reassured her. She knew she couldn't possibly ask for more. Even the grace she got felt undeserved.

But sometimes, when a new flower blossomed, pale and strange, unlike the rest, she would feel an ache she couldn't name. She'd touch its petals, lean close, try to summon a sound that felt right. The word would form in her throat, trembling, almost alive, and then vanish. Her mouth would close around silence.

Adam would see her furrowed brow and come to kneel beside her.

"It's an orchid," he'd say gently, mistaking her frustration for confusion.

Eve would nod, softening her face for him, and repeat it. "Orchid."

The sound settled like a stone in her chest.

She sometimes wanted to be open and share her deepest thoughts, but she feared that he'd think her ungrateful.

Soon he had escorted her out of her garden and towards their abode. Sometimes they simply slept wherever the stars met them. This was one such night.

They lay beneath the canopy of stars. Adam's arm draped across her waist, heavy and warm. He would whisper the day into her ear, how he'd watched the eagle hunt, or how the grapes grew sweeter by the hour. His words were always full of what *was*. Never of what *might be*.

She loved the sound of his voice, its rhythm more than its meaning. Sometimes she would close her eyes and let the syllables wash over her until they blurred into something like music.

Still, there were moments when she caught herself wondering.

Why was there only day and night? Could there not be something in between, something to name that soft half-light, a place for both rest and waking?
Why did the rivers only run one way? Did they never

wish to turn back, to see where they had come from?

Once, she had asked.

Adam smiled at her the way one might smile at a child. "There is no need for something in between," he said. "When everything is perfect." And she had nodded. He had almost the same response for everything, it was perfect the way it was. But she saw the sense in that. If all things in paradise were right, surely it was her thoughts that must be wrong?

But sometimes, when he slept beside her, his breath slow and even, she lay awake and listened to the silence. The garden was still, but not empty. There was a hum beneath the quiet, like a heartbeat too deep to hear.

The vines above her rustled softly though there was no wind.

She told herself it was nothing.

Yet in the moments before dawn, when the world was neither night nor day, she felt something stir within her chest. Not sorrow. Not fear. A kind of restlessness that rose and fell like a tide without a moon to command it.

It wasn't disobedience, she told herself. It was gratitude, so full it had nowhere to go.

That was the best she could make of it, unwilling to see herself as rebellious or unsatisfied with the order of things.

And yet, sometimes, she thought she could hear the garden breathe back.

One afternoon, while foraging, she felt a change. The air thickened, fragrant, heavy with the smell of something blooming unseen. The bees had gone quiet. She straightened, her heart fluttering, and looked toward the line of trees where the light turned darker, greener, towards the edge of the Eden she knew.

For a moment she thought she heard a voice, low and melodic, almost like laughter carried from far away. It sucked her in, threatening to take charge of her feet and direct her toward the recesses of Eden. But when she blinked, the sound was gone, and Adam was calling her name.

She bit her lower lip, wondering if what she had heard was true, or just another figment of her imagination that should be subdued.

"EVE!" Adam called out again with more urgency. She could tell he was getting more worried, although she couldn't quite fathom what he sought to protect her from. She was in Eden and nothing could harm her.

She started in the direction of his voice. After a few minutes' walk, his sturdy frame came into view.

"I'm right here." Eve consoled, fruit and edible plants in her hands, and said nothing of what she heard moments ago.

"It has been too long since I last laid eyes on you." He whined.

"I had only been away barely a day."

"It didn't feel that way to me," he said, pulling her

into an embrace.

Eve plastered a smile on her face. One of many masks she often had to wear, although she had no idea why. All she knew was it pleased him, and she was happy to please him. He stroked her hair for a little while, then released her.

"Come, let me tell you about my day." He said.

Eve looked at him considering telling him about the laughter she had heard from deep within the forest. Unsure how he'd react, she decided against it.

"Did something new happen today?" She asked, hopeful.

It didn't.

As the stars came out that night, she watched their reflections ripple across the pool beside them. Adam spoke of the work he'd done, of the creatures he'd named, of how good it all was. She leaned her head against his shoulder and listened, smiling where he could see it.

And when he said, "You make Eden complete," she believed him… almost.

His words carried on in a familiar tune. And soon those words gave way to actions.

As his hands found her supple breasts, softly grazing over her hardening nipples. He craved her body, and could hardly think of else when they were close. She reveled the way she made him feel. A man who was in charge of the whole world, helpless against her beauty. He squeezed her breast slightly, and then he moved on, dragging her hand to his erection. Eve did not resist.

"You do want me? He rasped.

"I do. I always do," Eve whispered, wrapping her small fingers around him.

Sometimes he couldn't wait to be inside her. Sometimes he was satisfied with the pleasure just her hands or mouth could bring. Eve tightened her grip around the soft outer layer of his growing erection, moving it up and down at a steady pace. Soon, he was moving his hips in sync with her hand.

Before long, his movements became irregular, more urgent and hungrier.

She could see the hunger in his eyes, and so she lowered her lips to the head of his manhood.

He was strong and she was frail in comparison, but when he was in her mouth like this. Suddenly she held all the power as he lost his ability to think of anything but her lips sliding up and down his shaft.

"Eve," he growled, sounding more beast than man. She persisted, bobbing her head faster, and feeling his hips meet her halfway, before losing control. She swallowed him whole, and he groaned through his climax. Spilling his seed down her throat, which she greedily devoured. He gasped and shuddered as she finally released him.

She secretly hated the taste, but didn't want hm to know.

When Adam regained the ability to form words, he

whispered with a voice drowning in sleep. "I thank God everyday for giving you to me. I can't imagine a life without you."

THREE

At the heart of the garden, it stood: the tree whose fruit shimmered as though secrets moved just beneath its skin.

It was not taller than the others, nor broader in it's reach, yet every path in the garden seemed to eventually curve back toward it. It was such that you could always locate it, no matter where you were. From this tree, Eden spiraled outward in every direction. Abundance radiating and fanning out farther than the eyes could behold. Ironic it was, that a few radius around the tree itself, life seemed to be mostly inexistent.

No bird perched in its branches, no beast grazed in its shade, and vines dared not cling to it. Even the wind, playful elsewhere, stilled around it, as if afraid to disturb what it did not understand.

Perhaps this was because it had the power to take and

never give back. Or perhaps it was its awry appearance.

The tree's trunk was wrong. Its bark was deep and furrowed. Not with the natural spiral of growth, but as if it was twisted out of rage by some unseen hands. Twisted until the trunk almost gave way, but just managed to stay rooted in the barren ground around it.

But the fruit? They were stark in contrast. They had the color of the sunset and the sunrise meeting, embodied in a rounded shape that beckoned on your innate desires. The first time the smell of the fruit wafted to her nose, she knew she did not recognize it as any other fruit growing in Eden. But the smell was so strong, she could nearly taste it on her tongue. She shivered, overcome by the desire to sink her teeth into the fleshy fruit. Eve shook her head to break free of the abominable thoughts.

Adam had told Eve of the sole law spoken by God upon his creation.

It was not written. It didn't have to be.
She heard it in his voice, weighty with the certainty of one who had heard it from God himself.

"You may eat freely of every tree in the garden,"
he recited, *"but of the tree of knowledge of good and evil, you shall not eat.*
For in the day you eat of it, you shall surely die."

He spoke the words as one might speak of the rising sun, an unchangeable truth.
Eve listened, and obeyed.

Though she passed it often. She never touched it. But

sometimes her eyes lingered, like they did today.
Not in defiance, but in wonder.

Why that tree?
Why place it in the center, where every path led back
to it?
And *what kind of knowledge could make the act of*
knowing it a sin?

When she asked Adam, he pursed his lips and
narrowed his eyes slightly, as if deciding how
concerned he should be at her questioning.

"Because obedience is part of faith," he told her. "We
must trust that what we are given is enough."
He meant it gently, and she wanted to believe him.

Yet the command had been spoken before her first
breath, before her voice, and still it shaped the edges
of her world.

There was no shame in Eden.
They moved naked and unhidden beneath the gaze of
heaven. Their bodies required no protection in
paradise. They bared themselves with no discomfort
or insecurity.

There was no sin, they laid together freely and often.
Though Adam assured her it was the most natural
thing in the world to desire sex, just as she had seen
many animals around them do. That only seemed to
increase her concern that he often seemed to desire it
more than she did. Eve tried to reach the same level of
enthusiasm during their congress, but to her it often

ended up feeling like a ritual to appease him or pass the time. It always ended in only his groans, and as abruptly as it began.

Eve took her pleasure where she could find it.

Where he grew more aroused, she found pride in causing it. Where he found the uncontrolled flow of his blood to his manhood, she found the intoxicating control in driving his need to culmination. And where he found the mind-numbing burst of pleasure as his muscles went rigid with climax, she found *nothing*.

Nothing that she felt when his mouth met hers with exuberant need, when he played and teased and fondled her breasts, or when he drove his hard length into her core that could compare to the release he seemed to feel when brought to that precipice.

On this night, he found her beneath the canopy of the date palms, where the air was warm and fragrant with honey and ripe fruit.

Adam kissed her in the way he often did, as if she belonged to him. And she let him believe it. She let him believe a lot when he held her like this.

His hands were sure, calloused from climbing trees. He held her hips as if he had shaped them himself and pulled her flush against his exposed groin. Instantly he began to grow harder against her buttocks. And she let her back mold to his hard chest and dropped her head back onto his shoulder in surrender. He moaned softly and slid one of his hands from her hip up to her stomach pulling her tighter against him as if trying to return her to himself.

She gasped slightly as his mouth traced the hollow of her throat, his hand slowly descending once more. This time his fingers found the course dark hair between her legs. He let his fingers run through her bush like the rivers though the meadows of Eden, until they found the crevice beneath. Eve's breath caught as his rough fingers trailed over the small spot at the top. A spot she had no name for. But just as quickly as the sensation hit her, it left as it so often did as he continued to insert two fingers into her. Eve tried to rock her hips backward to bring him back to the spot he had brushed over, but he just felt her buttocks push back against him and took it as invitation to continue on. He plunged his fingers deeper, in and out of her without reprieve.

"Do you like it?" he asked eagerly.

She nodded quickly and his lips curled with satisfaction. The truth was she didn't much like nor dislike it. It just felt life fingers moving inside her.

"We could do this every day…forever, just me and you." he whispered. Then in one swift movement, lifted her like she weighed nothing.

She had no idea why, but his words scared her. Forever was a very long time and she wasn't sure this was how she wanted to spend it.

He brought them down to the moss-covered ground

and bent her over onto her hands and knees. And pressed down on her back until her breasts nearly touched the ground. Then he planted both hands firmly on her hips again. His eyes landed on her glistening folds, now prominently displayed, as the rush of blood to his manhood intensified.
Patience was a virtue he could no longer afford. He positioned himself at her entrance.

"You are mine." He blurted through shallow breath as his need grew. "Given to me by God, nothing can take you from me."

"I am yours," she agreed. She knew that much. That she existed only because he prayed for it.

At her words, he groaned. And thrust deep inside her. She was tighter around him, as moisture had barely begun to gather there.

He was strong and knew it. When he moved above her, it was with the confidence of one who had named everything in sight, including her.

She moaned in response, but not for him alone. For the heat she was building inside herself, for the rhythm he didn't realize she was directing from him with the arch of her back as she rubbed that sensitive spot against his thrusting length as he moved.

He grew impatient, she knew she would never be able to focus on the teasing of that sacred spot long enough, while knowing what he wanted so badly. And so she relented, abandoning her fight for pleasure. Letting him pound into her.

As much as Eve tried to think of him inside her and feel the same growing arousal, she couldn't help but feel it only as an intrusion. And she let her body move automatically in response like so many times before. Eager to see him finish.

At least in bringing him to this ultimate pleasure, in watching him be rendered senseless, she could feel something else. Pride.

He groaned her name like a prayer. And stilled on a thrust as he emptied himself inside her, collapsing against her back. She said nothing. Only let him begin to soften inside her before she pulled away and let him fall from her again. They both moved to sit facing each other.

The garden resumed its slow, drowsy hum. Adam smiled, peaceful, certain of their shared contentment.

Eve smiled back, gentle, practiced.

He slept quickly, limbs loose in satisfaction.

She lay awake beside him, eyes tracing the slow rhythm of light filtering through the palm fronds. The sweetness of fruit and sweat clung to her skin until it became almost cloying.

Across the clearing, in the distance, the forbidden tree caught her eye. Its fruit glimmered faintly, each orb pulsing as though alive. She imagined she could feel that pulse against her ribs.

The leaves rustled. Perhaps it was only the wind. Perhaps it was something listening, or a silent affirmation of her thoughts.

Eve turned onto her side and pressed closer to Adam's warmth, seeking the safety she had come to know at his side. And drifting off to the hollow feeling that often mirrored his afterglow.

Another night in paradise.

FOUR

The first dream came on a moonless night.

The night was alive, filled with a cacophony of noise, the nightingale's song, the cricket chirp, the owl's hoot and a litany of other nocturnal animals. Eve had always believed those animals to be shy.

They never came out during the day, only when the sky was blanketed with darkness and others were fast asleep. They needed the world to themselves. She had never even seen some of them, and imagined Adam must have stayed up night after night to name them.

Sometimes his determination and commitment were admirable.

Millions of stars speckled the sky above them. They were just as shy as the animals, some shining brighter than others. Adam had told her that God had made the sun, the moon, and the stars. The sun to rule by day, the moon and stars by night. The moon was bold on some nights, others it disappeared, giving way to only the stars.

Eve lay curled in the cool hush of their sleeping grove, Adam's arm draped heavy across her hip, the slow rise and fall of his breath brushing her shoulder. And yet, though her body rested beside him, her spirit drifted elsewhere.

She stood on a path in the forest, one she knew.

It was the path to the right, the one she had never ventured down. Now she let her feet carry her on. The path seemed to just go on forever, despite her steady pace forward, she wasn't seeming to get closer to the end.

She paused and looked toward the heavens.

The sky above her was velvet; dark, deep, pulsing with unfamiliar constellations. Stars beat like distant hearts. The wind now carried no scent of Eden, but hummed with a rhythm that felt older than the world she knew.

Eve looked back down the path ahead of her and gasped. Now paralyzed.

In the distance, a figure stood in the middle of the path with her back to Eve. It was Eve's figure.

But Not Eve's.
Not quite.

She had the shape of one made of Adam's rib. The curves of body clear from here.

Her long ebony hair spilled like waves of ink down a

back of bronze skin, darker and richer in tone than Eve's own. She looked carved from shadow and starlight both.

Eve noticed movement at her feet. A serpent creature unlike she had ever seen slithered there. It moved like it had no bones, and nothing to propel it forward, and still it coiled around her smoothly.

Eve didn't know whether to be mesmerized or cautious.

Eve called out.

The woman began to turn. Eve felt the air swell, felt recognition bloom like fire in her chest.

But before she could see her face, she woke with a sharp inhale, a trembling ache low in her belly. Her face was moistened with sweat and her heart thudded violently in her chest.

Adam stirred, murmured her name in his sleep, tightened his arm around her and settled again.

Eve said nothing.

In the days that followed, she wandered more. Unable to fully wake from her dream.

Each new spring she found, she knelt beside and drank from it. Each hidden path she uncovered, she followed. When she stumbled onto unfamiliar clearings, she lay in the grass with her eyes closed and let the sun warm the soft places of her body until she swore, she could hear the earth humming beneath her spine.

Discovering new parts of Eden felt like discovering new parts of herself.

In a way it made her understand Adam more. What a thrill it was to discover new parts of yourself and have dominion over those parts.

Sometimes her wandering carried her so far, she did not return to their sleeping grove before nightfall. When she slipped back into Adam's arms late, or even at dawn, he greeted her with gentle confusion, soft concern, and a warmth that felt like a hand guiding her back to the familiar.

The second dream came after a day like this.

Again, she drifted into a place she had never walked while awake.

This place felt older.
Vaster.
Towering trees rose in thick columns around it; their trunks braided with vines and heavy with moss. Roots arched up from the earth like the backs of sleeping beasts, disappearing into fern-laced undergrowth. The canopy above was layered and dense, filtering sunlight into shifting ribbons of emerald and gold that drifted across bark and water alike.

A pool shimmered beneath the canopy, murky green blue, rimmed with slick black stones. Drops of water fell from the foliage above and kissed its surface in soft, rhythmic pulses, sending ripples outward. Vines trailed low enough to brush the water, and when disturbed, faint luminescent algae glowed beneath the surface, a hidden light awakening at the slightest touch.

Eve found herself at the edge of that pool, now dark as polished onyx.

Her reflection shimmered on the black surface.

But the woman looking back was not her.

The face was not hers.
The eyes burned like darkening dusk, where Eve's were like the amber stone. Her face was sharper but feminine.
This mouth curled in defiance, in invitation, in knowing.

Eve reached toward the water. But the reflection did not mimic her movements.

Instead, the woman in the pool moved on her own, slowly running her hand down the full curves of her own body, as though savoring her own shape. As the strange woman in the water traced her heavy breasts, causing her dark nipples to pebble beneath her touch. Her hand continued its path down her soft voluptuous curves until her fingers found their way to the soft mound between her legs. Eve stopped breathing, as she watched those fingers dip through her dark hair to disappear inside her slowly, only to emerge glistening with moisture as if she had dipped them in the pool.
She began a rhythm of small strokes over that special spot only Eve seemed to notice, until now. As she increased her speed, her breast rose and fell at a similar pace. She touched herself with a reverence Eve had never felt for her own skin.

Eve could not take only watching anymore, she had to reach out once more. But when her fingers got close to the surface, she was ripped from her slumber, breathing heavily, once again slick with sweat, her hands clenched in the grass.

She did not sleep again that night.

CHAPTER

FIVE

The following day, Eve wandered farther than she had ever dared.

Down the unfamiliar path to the right. The one that called her. The one from her dream.

The farther she went down the path, navigating the overwhelming thicket, the stranger things looked. The familiar terrain of Eden, the gentle orchards, the sunlit springs, the winding paths she could walk with her eyes closed fell away behind her. She moved without thinking, her feet guided more by memory of her dreams than by the lay of the land.

She pushed on until she reached the edge of the Eden they knew. But to her surprise, the path didn't end there.

The path curved gently beneath an arch of interwoven vines, the greenery bending inward as though in quiet invitation. Sunlight filtered through the layered canopy in fractured beams, casting shifting gold across the narrow trail. Leaves brushed against one another overhead, forming a living tunnel that breathed with the faintest wind. The ground was damp but firm, scattered with fallen petals and soft fragments of leaf. It felt less like something carved by feet and more like something parted by intention.

The air hit her first. Heavier here. So thick she thought she might be able to reach out and grab a fistful. And the lush garden here seemed to thrive, drinking it in.

Then she smelt the sweetness of figs.
Sweet, heavy, ripe in a way that did not belong to this part of the garden.
The fragrance curled around her like a beckoning hand.

Eve followed.

And soon she came to something familiar in this strange place.

Her breath caught.

It was the pool from her dream.

Her body reacted before her mind caught up, heat blooming, breath faltering, something within her clenching tight as memory and want collided. The air tasted the way the dream had tasted: sweet, forbidden, inevitable.

Her knees were weak. Whether from the long walk, or the revelation, she didn't know.

Thankfully, she found a stone that appeared made for

resting. She sat upon the elevated flat stone at the water's edge. It was warm beneath her, as though someone had just been there.

Her mind swam with memories of the dream that took place here. And then without planning, without fear, without thought, she lay back on the stone, letting the strange wildness of this place sweep through her.

Bringing her own hand to her breast. Just as she had seen the figure in her dream do. She hesitantly ran her finger around her nipple, getting closer in smaller circles until she flattened two fingers against her nipple and found it hardened as if kissed by cold air, even though her flesh was burning. Her hand began to squeeze and knead her breast. It felt different than what she was used to. As the other hand started to slide down her stomach to her hot wet center. Just as the dream woman had done. She moved her fingers until she found the spot she craved. She let out a small gasp at the sensation, and stroked her finger back and forth, then in small circles, testing the different movements. She felt the small bud swell beneath her teasing fingers.

As her pace and breathing quickened, and her head fell further back with eyes tightly closed. Eve felt something in her building, she felt soon she might come apart. Then suddenly she moaned loudly and arched her back, unable to help herself, only able to feel the intense bursting pleasure in her. She rode it in descending waves.

She barely had time to lower her back to the stone and drop her hand from her still pulsing center, when she felt another hand replace her own, cupping her still throbbing core.

A softer hand than Adam's.
It was Warm.
It was Certain.

The palm pressing gently against the center of her pleasure, echoing the throb in her chest.

Eve's eyes flew open.

A woman leaned over her, close enough that Eve could feel her breath on her cheek. Her hair fell like a curtain of night, darker and in softer waves than the tight curls Eve had. Her cheekbones were sharp, regal, as if sculpted to defy her softness. Her skin warm bronze, smooth and alive. And her smile.

Her smile was the one from the dream.
Defiant.
Knowing.
Beautiful.

The woman's eyes were deep and curious, the color of burning dusk.

Eve's voice failed her.

The stranger tilted her head, amusement curling the corner of her mouth, as if she had been waiting a very long time to be seen.

"Hello, Eve," she murmured.

Her voice was velvet and shadow.
A voice as old as Eden.
A voice that tasted like figs on the tongue.

"I wondered how long it would take you to find me."

CHAPTER

SIX

The woman leaning over her was radiant. She wore the desert like a second skin, warm, wind-kissed, carrying the scent of damp earth and something faintly sweet, like crushed petals hidden under sand. Her thick dark hair framed a face built of sharp angles and quiet strength. Her gaze was intense, unwavering, as though she saw both the surface and the secret beneath it.

There was a natural command in the way she held herself: shoulders straight, chin lifted, the slight narrowing of her eyes betraying a mind always working. Though naked, like Eve, she was adorned in layered strands of carved stone and bone which rested against her collarbones with the weight of stories. When she moved, the ornaments whispered as if telling them.

Her beauty was not gentle. It struck, like a thorn, like hunger, like need.

Her dark eyes locked onto Eve's, and the garden around them shivered, as if recognizing a power older than its own roots.

"You're not Adam," Eve whispered.

She tried to sit up, though her limbs trembled with something wholly new.
Not fear.
Something deeper.

The woman's smile formed slowly, knowingly.
"No," she said. "And you… are not his shadow."

Her voice was low and rich, warm enough to melt stone. Eve felt the echo of that voice ripple over her skin. Her scalp prickled. Her breath hitched. Her pulse beat in places she had not known pulses lived.

"Who are you?" Eve asked.

Eve finally managed to push herself off the stone. The woman leaned back to give her room but continued to watch her like a hawk watches it's prey. It made Eve aware of her nakedness in a way she had never been.

"I am the one who named herself," the woman replied, her pride soft as velvet and sharp as truth. "And I named this place into being."

She reached up, plucked a hidden fruit Eve had never seen from the tree above them, and bit into it. Juice slid down her fingers, glowing like garnet in the strange half-light.

"Only Adam can name," Eve said quietly, though even as the words left her lips, they felt unsure.

The woman laughed, not cruelly, but with a heat that curled through the air.
"Adam names what is given," she said.
"I name what I desire to give."

Eve struggled to understand. "I have tried to name things I grew in the garden; I could not speak them." Eve confided.

She regarded Eve closely, as if deciding how much to say. "Perhaps it was because you believed yourself incapable more than you believed the names."

A thrill ran through Eve, bright as sunrise and dark as the pool beside them. *Could she really name? Did this woman think her capable of such a gift?*

She turned fully toward the woman, her body responding before her mind dared.

"I think I know you," Eve breathed excitedly. "I dreamt of you... And this place."

"This is a place born of longing," the woman said. "Not unlike you, Eve."

The truth in those words struck deep. Eve swallowed, her hands trembling against the stone.

"Dreams are a good place for the mind to reach for desires they resist in waking hours." The woman explained easily.

"You dream too?" Eve asked curiously.

"You seem surprised," she said smiling kindly, "Do you and Adam not talk about dreams?"

"Adam doesn't dream." Eve stated plainly.

The woman paused, considering that, then nodded. "I can't say I am too surprised by that."

Eve looked to the floor as she pondered those words. She seemed to know Adam well. But how? Adam and Eve were alone.

"Eve, let me ask you…" The woman spoke, interrupting Eve's thoughts, "If Adam did not teach you about dreams, and you did not name them, how did you know what to call it?"

Eve thought about that now. She had been so caught up in the nature of the dreams before, she hadn't thought of that. After she began dreaming, she just knew it.

"I don't know." She finally admitted.

"Interesting." The woman said, clearly thinking about something deeply.

"Will you teach me your name?" Eve asked, nervously now.

The woman's eyes turned back to Eve's and softened with something like triumph, or tenderness.

"Lilith."

Eve repeated it instinctively, as she had repeated every name Adam had ever taught her.
But this name was different.
It did not pass through her like a borrowed word.
It landed.
Rooted.

Bloomed.

The ground trembled beneath them.
White orchids burst into blossom at the base of the rock, pale, soft, trembling petals unfurling as though waking from centuries of sleep.

Eve gasped, tearing her gaze from Lilith to the sudden blooms.

"Did you bring those into being? I know these flowers. I grow them in my garden. They are my favorite"

Lilith's smile brightened, sharp and tender both.

"And you grew them here, too. I did not name them, and they have never bloomed in this place before now."

She gestured toward the flowers, the dark pool, the trembling vines.
"As a part of your longing is quenched, this place of longing grows."

She leaned closer.
"It was your longing, Eve. Your flowers. Your desire. Your creation."

Eve stared at her, stunned. The meaning rippled through her like warm water.

Lilith tilted her head, her smile turning playful, wicked, unbearably intimate.

"My question is…" she murmured, dark lashes lowering.
"Was it my name that eased your longing…"

She reached up and brushed a strand of hair from Eve's cheek with a featherlight touch.

"…or what I felt beneath my palm moments ago?"

CHAPTER

SEVEN

Eve returned just before dawn. The moon had long disappeared and now the darkness began to fade, making way for the rising sun.

Somehow, she had lost track of time and had stayed away longer than she should have. Asking Lilith question after question, and Lilith patiently answered them all.

Though there were still some questions Eve had been afraid to ask.

The Garden looked the same. And that was the strangest part.
For Eve no longer felt the same in it.

She walked its familiar paths like a woman who had touched the edge of the map, where creation frays into myth and nothing is safe or certain anymore.

The morning light pressed through the trees in soft shafts. Birds trilled their usual melodies, yet something beneath it all felt skewed, as if Eden itself sensed that a piece of her had wandered beyond its bounds.

Dew caught in the hairs on her legs. The grass brushed her ankles with a familiar tenderness. But her skin felt different against the world now, as though the air recognized she had breathed another garden's breath.

"Lilith." Eve whispered, wanting to bring a little bit of her home with her. And the garden shuddered at her name. Trees rustled without wind, animals in the distance roared or whined.

From the first time she had seen her in her dream, she felt she would bring chaos. But she wasn't worried about the chaos that clung to Lilith like a second skin. What worried her, was how she was drawn to that chaos.

You are where you should be, Eve told herself. There was no fighting nature, especially if it was ordained by God.

She found Adam in a stream not far from where they most often slept.

He stood knee-deep, the muscles in his calves flexing beneath the clear current. The rising sun gilded his warm dark skin, turning him into a figure carved from honey and dawn. His face was tight, lips drawn, brow furrowed, as though his thoughts had been spiraling long before she arrived.

When he saw her, relief broke across his features like sunlight scattering the night.

Then came something else.
Not quite anger.
Not quite fear.
A suspicion sharp enough to cut.

"Where have you been?" he demanded.

The words struck her harder than she expected.

He had never used that tone with her, sharp, accusatory, edged with something almost brittle. And his eyes, dark and deep as the soil, held a storm she did not yet know how to weather.

For a heartbeat, she wondered, *Did he remember Lilith?*

Lilith had told her about their creation, and about her refusal to lie with Adam. But Eve had assumed the woman before her, the first woman, had been erased from his memory when she left. Why else had Adam never spoken her name? Never warned Eve she was not the first? Not alone.

But the look in his eyes now, the way his voice cracked on demand instead of plea, the way his posture braced as though expecting betrayal…

Perhaps he remembered more than either of them realized.
Not as fact, but as fear. A deep insecurity he never thought to name.

Perhaps he feared Eve might make the same choice Lilith had made before her.

And Eve, trembling from too many truths, knew she could not tell him the whole of anything.

She knelt beside the water, lowering her hands into the stream. The cold stole the warmth from her palms and washed away any lingering trace of figs she did not wish him to question.

"I couldn't sleep," she said lightly. "I walked."

Adam stepped out of the water and came to her side, the drops sliding down his legs catching the pale morning light.

He brushed a loose strand of hair behind her ear. His touch was gentle. Familiar. His voice softened instantly, as though he regretted how sharply the first words had fallen from him.

"I looked for you," he said. "I called your name."

"I wasn't far," she lied. "But I didn't hear you. I thought it best to sleep elsewhere, so my stirring wouldn't disturb you."

He crouched beside her, hands settling firmly on her arms, his grip warm and grounding and a little too tight.

"You should not go alone, Eve. There are places in the garden even I do not know. You could be hurt or…" His voice strained.
"…lost to me."

Something in his jaw worked, as though he was wrestling with a thought he didn't want to speak.
He swallowed thickly.

"The devil is cunning. It watches. Whispers. You must be careful what you listen to."

The words fell heavy between them. The weight of doubt.

Adam's words could be truth, but for some reason she knew them for what they were, just as she always knew him for what he was. He did not believe his own words.

It was not the Devil he feared. Eve was not even sure the devil he had described to her once was real.

Was it the name he gave the woman who dared name herself?

Maybe, he *had* told her about Lilith.

Just not by that name.

Her mind flashed with memory. The way Adam had described the devil once.

A creature haunting the edges of the garden.
Crafty. Rebellious. Fallen from God's grace when it defied him.

Could he really have been speaking of Lilith?

Had he replaced her divine name with a curse?
A name he could speak without remembering what he'd lost?
A name he could use to warn Eve of a freedom he himself feared?

Eve's heart hammered.

Lilith had left her mark.

Even stripped of her place in his story, she lingered in his words.

"I'm yours," Eve said softly, leaning closer, pressing her lips to his shoulder.

It wasn't meant as lie, but it felt like one.

The lie tasted bitter in her mouth. But she told it anyway.
She told it to protect him.
To protect herself.
To protect the fragile balance between them.

So, she leaned into Adam's warmth, letting his arm circle her shoulders. His breath brushed her temple. His body vibrated with relief.

"Eve," he sighed. "My Eve."

She let him say her name.
She let him believe it anchored her.

But as she looked out over Eden, she noticed things she had not seen before.

The river flowed a little too fast, as though uneasy. The birdsong faltered in places, like a voice catching on a secret it doesn't wish to tell.
Even the sunlight seemed thinner, fraying at the edges.

Eden, itself, sensed the crack forming in her. Or perhaps it sensed the truth growing in her chest.

She could play the role Adam needed.
She would play it well.

To save the perfect Eden she had always known.

CHAPTER

EIGHT

The next day, Eve went walking.

Not her normal meandering stroll through the citrus groves or along the riverbanks.
Not the familiar loops Adam could predict by heart.

She walked with purpose, with direction, with a newly born map inside her.
A private one.

She went to a place she knew Adam would not dare to look. She wished to be alone.

Past her garden, where the herbs she'd planted lifted their heads toward her like curious children.
Past the olive trees, where the branches always reached for her in greeting.
Past the glade where she and Adam had first lain beneath the stars.

Until she came to **the tree**.

The Tree of Knowledge of Good and Evil.

It stood tall and silent, towering like a pillar of breath held for centuries. Its fruit glowed faintly, as though lit from within by a buried sun. The hush around it was no longer ominous to her, it felt more like reverence now. Recognition. Invitation.

Curiosity did not frighten her as it once had.
Not since Lilith taught her what longing could build.
Not since she had tasted a different world and felt it thrum through her veins.

A world she couldn't forget, despite trying to do what was right. She still had so many questions for Lilith. So many things she wished to know of her world. Of her.

But to go back felt like a betrayal of Adam. And to forget, seemed like a betrayal of herself.

Adam never came here.
He feared what he did not understand.

But Eve…
Eve was learning to understand.

She approached the trunk with slow, steady steps.
The air around the tree parted for her like a veil drawn back.
The light dimmed and sharpened all at once, as if the world leaned in to listen.

"You know, don't you?" she whispered to the tree.

Her voice trembled, not from fear, but from awe.
She pressed her palm to the bark.

It was warm.

Not just sun-warm.
Alive-warm.

Above her, a rustle.
A shifting of weight.
Leaves trembling.

But not from the tree.

A serpent slid down the grooves of the bark, long and silver, scales etched with pale swirling patterns like written scripture made flesh. Light shimmered on its body like moonlight on water.

It did not strike.
It did not hiss.
It watched.

Eve knelt before it, instinctively.
Something inside her recognized this creature, not from sight, but from memory carried in her blood.

"You are hers, aren't you?" she whispered.

Serpents were of Lilith's making.
They never left her side in the wild garden born of longing.

The serpent lowered its head in acknowledgment, then slithered closer. Its movements were smooth, hypnotic, like liquid thought.

"You smell of her," it hissed out the words.

Its voice was low, thick, warm, like oil poured into water, spreading without sound.

Eve stared, shocked, as she understood the serpents' words. "You speak." She stammered.

"We all do, some just clearer than others. We were the first of her conjured companions, created out of her longing for answers. It was important we could give them." It offered explanation in its quiet hiss. "But she learn to speak to us all, learning is easier for one ready to listen."

"How are you here? In this part of the garden, I have not known serpents here before." Eve asked.

"I followed her scent." The serpent explained, tasting the air with its tongue.

Eve swallowed. "She is not here."

"She is." the serpent replied, curling its body beside Eve.
It slid in slow, thoughtful loops, forming lazy circles at the tree's base.

A tremor of uncontrollable excitement moved through Eve, and she spun her head from side to side in search of Lilith.

"We are creatures of Lilith's longing. We are drawn to it. And where you go, her longing now follows."

Eve's breath hitched.
Her throat tightened.

She closed her eyes, not to hide, but because the truth hurt and healed at the same time. She had been desperate to return to Lilith's garden, to fill her growing void. But was afraid Lilith cared not if she returned, for what could Eve offer that Lilith couldn't make for herself.

"I tried to forget," she whispered.
"To be content as I once thought I was."

The serpent's body shifted, like shadows brushing her skin.

"He wants the Eve he named," it said. "But that is not the only name you know now."

Her throat burned.
Her chest ached as though she'd swallowed a star.

Adam had given her a name of obedience.
Lilith was a name of desire.

Both lived inside her now.
Both fought for space.

Eve lifted her gaze.
The serpent lifted its head in mirrored motion.

Its eyes gleamed of ancient knowledge.

"Why don't you eat from this tree, Eve?" it asked curiously.

The question struck her and derailed her thoughts.

"I cannot," she answered quickly. "It is the only rule."

The serpent's coils tightened slightly, as if satisfied by her answer.

"Is it?" It hissed.

Eve's brows furrowed, and she nodded.

The serpent circled her once more, slow and

deliberate, like a thought taking shape.

"If it is the only rule," it said,
"then what rule keeps you from the taste of Lilith?"

The words sank into her like fangs.
Revelation its venom.

Temptation flooded her veins, warm and dizzying.

Eve felt something inside her release, the knot of fear,
the weight of purpose, the role she was meant to play.

The serpent bobbed its head once, in a bow or a
challenge, she wasn't sure.

As for her new direction, she was sure.

CHAPTER

NINE

Eve returned to Lilith's garden before the first color of sunset touched the sky.

The air here felt different, charged, expectant, alive. As if every leaf knew she was coming. As if the soil recognized the rhythm of her steps. Moss softened beneath her bare feet, humming faintly like breath drawn before a kiss.

Lilith stood at the center of her wild domain, half-shadowed, half-luminous, as though she belonged to both night and morning. She looked at Eve, and something in her eyes burned, knowledge or hunger or both. The kind of gaze that saw not skin or shape, but the soul.

Eve was now lost for words. She knew she had to find her but hadn't thought of what she would say when she did.

Finally, she blurted, "I came back."

Lilith smiled wide. "You did. Welcome back."

After a single shared heartbeat, Lilith closed the gap between them. Coming to stand before her. They stared into each other's eyes for a moment, thick which anticipation, both searching for something.

"What should we do today?" Lilith asked casually, breaking the silence.

Eve was ready for something, but not that. She laughed nervously. "I am not sure what I am supposed to say."

"You're not supposed to say anything. I am only asking what *you* would like to do?" Lilith assured.

There was a loaded pause. Eve's neck warmed and her mind raced with things she would like to do with Lilith. Things she wouldn't dare say out loud.

"Can you teach me to understand the animals, the way you do? Their words, I mean." Eve asked, deciding to go with her safer desire.

There was a momentary flash of something like disappointment in her eyes. But Lilith smiled softly. "I'd be honored."

They spent days together exploring Lilith's garden. Lilith taught Eve the names that lived there.

The animals Eve didn't know; large birds with glossy black wings that seemed to shimmer blue or green with movement, long haired goats with curling horning and long beards, and strong prowling cats like the lioness but black as night.

She learned them as ravens, goats, and panthers. And after learning their names, Lilith helped her learn their voices.

At night she would return to Adam, but her mind would not. Not fully. She would practice with the animals of Eden. And as soon as she was able she would return to Lilith with the first light, to learn more.

Beyond the land, it's flora and fauna. She was learning Lilith.

The same way she observed and studied Adam to know his whims. She studied Lilith, to learn her heart.

Eve noticed that Lilith never lingered long where tenderness threatened to root. She was generous with knowledge, patient in her instruction, her hands steady as she guided vine and thorn into place.

But when laughter rose too freely between them, when silence softened into something warmer, Lilith would shift. A half-step back. A turned shoulder. A redirection toward the soil, the weather, the structure of things.

She spoke of solitude without bitterness, yet never of loneliness. She offered fruit, shelter, insight, but never the unguarded center of herself. It was not coldness. It was preservation. Lilith held her power the way one holds a blade; not to wound, but to ensure no one could wound her first.

Never again would she let someone try to take something from her. Everything she gave, she gave willingly, of her own power.

The river ran quieter in this part of Lilith's garden, its surface broken only by drifting leaves and the slow turning of light beneath it. Lilith knelt at the bank, hands submerged as she washed soil from a cluster of uprooted herbs. Eve settled beside her in the grass, close enough that their knees nearly aligned, but not touching.

Lilith had not really touched her since the first time they met.

Lilith worked with deliberate precision. She separated root from stem, laid each piece in orderly rows. Her movements were efficient, practiced. Controlled.

"You pull too quickly," she said without looking up.

Eve leaned forward. "Show me."

Lilith shifted closer. She reached for Eve's wrist to guide her grip, but stopped just shy of contact.

"Like this," she murmured, adjusting the angle of Eve's hand with her own hovering beside it.

Their fingers grazed at the same root at once.

The contact was brief. Accidental enough to deny. Deliberate enough to feel.

Eve didn't withdraw.

Lilith noticed.

She moved behind Eve then, repositioning to

demonstrate more clearly. Her knees pressed into the grass at either side of Eve's hips, not touching, but close enough that Eve felt surrounded by warmth.

"Twist before you lift," Lilith said. "Let it come to you, don't force it."

Her breath traced the back of Eve's neck as she leaned forward, hands braced in the earth on either side of Eve's own. Lilith's breasts now pressing at her back. The air between them thinned.

Eve could feel the tension in Lilith's shoulders, the way strength lived there even at rest.

"You carry it differently," Eve said quietly.

Lilith stilled. "Carry what?"

"Being alone."

The river kept moving. A bird called from somewhere distant.

Lilith's voice lowered when she answered. "Alone is lighter than dependence, then submission."

It was not sharp. It was practiced.

Eve turned her head slightly, not enough to close the space, but enough to see the curve of Lilith's mouth. It almost softened. Almost curved upward. But something caught it before it could complete the motion.

Restraint.

Eve did not flinch at Lilith's closeness. Did not recoil from the steadiness of her presence behind her. She remained still, listening as if Lilith's quieter tones mattered more than her words.

Lilith's hands shifted in the soil again. Close to Eve's hips now. Close enough that if either of them leaned a fraction of an inch, the space would vanish.

"You don't turn from my touch," Lilith observed aloud.

Eve's pulse beat hard in her throat. "No."

Another pause.

Lilith's shoulders eased, just slightly, but enough that her breast shifted against Eve's back. Soliciting a reaction from her that she had no control over, and she nearly gave in to it.

When she stepped away, the air felt abruptly colder.

She resumed kneeling at Eve's side rather than behind her. Safe distance restored. Composure reclaimed.

But Eve had felt it, that almost-smile, that guarded breath faltering, that moment where Lilith forgot to retreat quickly enough.

And Lilith had felt it too.

Eve did not pull away.
Eve did not tremble.
Eve stayed.

The river kept moving, patient and unhurried, as if it knew the boundary between them would not hold forever.

Not like this.

TEN

Eve woke with Adam's arms around her in their usual spot beneath the willows. Where she normally found comfort in the rise and fall of his broad chest at her back. This morning, it was stifling.

She wriggled out of his arms and rose for the day quietly so as not to disturb him.

Outside Adam's embrace, the garden breathed.

Mist curled low to the earth, sliding over her ankles like affectionate spirits. The air smelled of citrus blossoms and honey. She braided her thick honey curls with sprigs from her garden, mint, lavender, rosemary. Her fingers moving with practiced ease. The herbs released their fragrance under her touch, blessing her hair with the scent of the earth.

She hummed as she worked the soil.

Her garden, the one shaped by her own hands, always gave her a peace the rest of Eden could not. It felt like a small truth carved into the world, a corner that answered to her alone. The dirt clung to her fingers like memory, cool and rich, as though it recognized her skin.

The squash vines had begun curling around the base of her feet, their flowers opening in slow, languid sighs. The vines had spread farther than she planted them, wandering in curious, unbound spirals.

"Grow where you wish," she whispered. "One of us ought to."

The petals opened wider, as if in agreement.

Lilith had taught her how to speak to the things that grow in Eden, just like the animals that inhabit it, not to command them but to *listen*. How to hear their responses not in words but in movement, in bloom, in the subtle shift of breath around them.

Eve never saw Eden as dominion.
Not the way Adam did.

She saw it as communion.

Later, she sat on the bank of the river, humming the tune she had learned from the finches. The sound skipped across the water. A small turtle paddled by, blinking slowly up at her.

"You hum too fast," the turtle remarked.

Eve smiled. "And you move too slow."

The turtle hoisted itself onto a sun-warmed stone protruding from the water.

"I still got where I was going, didn't I?" it replied.

"Fair enough," she laughed, tossing a pebble into the stream.

A rustle overhead signaled the arrival of another visitor. A chimp dropped from a branch with theatrical flair and landed beside her, immediately combing its fingers through her braids. Eve leaned into the grooming, comforted by the intimacy of it. They had always tended one another, but now she understood the gestures. Now, thanks to Lilith's teachings, nothing stood between their meanings.

"Adam's brooding again," the chimp warned, parting one braid to pick a leaf from it. "His discontent disturbs the birds, they scatter from him when he is like this. Of course, he is only recently like this."

Eve sighed. "He is bothered that I busy myself more with the garden, with you all… and less with him."

The chimp made an amused clicking sound. "I don't think it's *us* he's worried about you getting too close to."

Eve's heart fluttered.
She turned her head to glance back at her primate friend. "You know about *her*?"

"We remember her," it said simply.
"We were here first."

Eve's mind reeled. The significance of that, of the beasts having known Lilith before Adam named them, made her chest ache.

The chimp continued, still picking gently at her braid.

"She was funny, you know? Clever. She made jokes Adam didn't get. He begrudged her for it. That she didn't shape her laughter around him. But she made *us* howl."

Eve's heart warmed, the ache turning tender.

"We taught her to climb trees," it added proudly. "She wasn't very good. Her feet weren't made for it. But that never stopped her."

Eve laughed softly, leaning her cheek against the chimp's furry head. "I would have liked to see that."

"When you began speaking to us the way she had," it said, voice dropping, "we knew she had been found. And found someone who could laugh with her."

Eve beamed, warmth blooming under her ribs. But beneath that warmth lay something heavier, doubt.

Doubt that she could return to Adam as she had been. Doubt that she could unlearn the things Lilith had awoken in her.
Doubt that the ache inside her could be soothed by anything but Lilith.

But she must.
She had to try.

So she sat with her primate friend in silence awhile, both of them looking out over the river. The world felt suspended, caught between what it had been and what it was becoming.

That night, she went to Adam willingly. She kissed his throat. Pressed herself against him beneath the olive trees, hands exploring, breath soft.

He responded with the hunger she knew he would. He held her tight like she was a gift he feared losing. Hands firm, voice low with praise.

Eve let herself be pulled into the moment, closed her eyes, and tried to feel that small pleasure she knew possible with him. The satisfaction of satisfying him so completely. The sense of power in pushing him to the brink of euphoria.

But her body didn't burn the way it had under Lilith's mere gaze. There was some pleasure, yes. But it was like eating without hunger.

Still, she gave him what he needed.

And afterward, he held her as though she were the axis of the world.

"Oh, I have a gift for you!" Adam said breaking the silence as they lay there.

He released her from his embrace and rose to his feet eagerly. She took her time getting to her feet.

"What is it?"

"Follow me, I will show you."

He took her hand and led her around the willows. She wasn't quite sure what she was looking at. He had taken branches and bent them into shape, secured with vines, until they formed a small enclosure.

In it was a small bird flitting about, from side to side.

She looked a Adam in confusion. He looked so proud of himself, but Eve wasn't. She couldn't fathom why he would build something like that.

"I call it a cage. You have been away so much, you weren't here when I named this one. So I kept it for you." He explained his gift, "So you could learn."

Eve stared at him and back at the small bird in its cage. Was this really because of her?

"Thank you," she said hesitantly, "I have seen it now, tell me its name, and we will let it go."

Adam's face fell. Clearly displeased by her lack of enthusiasm.

"Why let it go? We can make it happier. Give it food, so it no longer has to find its own. Whatever it needs."

It didn't seem happier. It did not speak to her, it sang no song. But she feared arguing with Adam would make her seem ungrateful.

She also feared leaving for so long again. How many more animals would wait, caged, for her to learn.

ELEVEN

Eve entered Lilith's garden when the sun had already begun it's descent. She had not meant for the visit to be brief. But Adam had found her, while she tended her caged friend, the need in him clear.

There was still the faint scent of Adam's hands on her skin.

Lilith noticed it immediately. And tried to hide her disdain.

"You do not stay long anymore," she said, not accusing. Simply stating.

"I come when I can," Eve replied.

Lilith's jaw tightened almost imperceptibly. "When you *can*, not when you *want*?"

"I want to come whenever I can." Eve insisted.

Lilith turned fully toward her then. "You speak as though you are choosing between orchards."

Eve's chin lifted. "I am choosing."

"Are you?" Lilith stepped closer, not enough to touch, but enough to press the air thin between them. "Or do you return to him because it is easier to be kept than to be known?"

Heat flared in Eve's chest.

"I don't belong to him."

Lilith's eyes darkened. "Yet you carry his scent with you still."

Eve should have stepped back.

She didn't.

Instead, she moved forward.

Their bodies nearly touching.

"If I remain," Eve said, voice steady, "it is because I am deciding. Not because I am kept."

She was trying to veil the chord Lilith was striking. She had no idea about the caged bird, and how she exemplified it.

Something flickered across Lilith's face, anger, yes. But beneath it, something more fragile.

Lilith lifted her hand.

For a breath, Eve thought she would push her away.

Instead, Lilith's fingers closed around Eve's chin, not harshly, not cruelly, but with unmistakable intention. She tilted Eve's face upward.

"So, you *choose* to be claimed," Lilith challenged.

Her voice had lowered, that quiet register that carried challenge and heat beneath it.

Eve's pulse hammered, but she did not break eye contact.

"Not by him."

The words barely rose above breath.

Lilith's grip did not tighten, but it did not release. Her eyes flared, emboldened.

Their foreheads drifted close enough that Eve could feel the warmth of Lilith's skin without contact. Breath mingled. Shared. Slow.

Eve could see the restraint gathering in Lilith's shoulders again, the same tension she wore like armor.

Lilith's thumb shifted.

It brushed Eve's lower lip, deliberate, exploratory.

Testing.

Eve's mouth parted slightly without thinking.

The air changed. There was no innocence left in the space between them now. Only awareness. Raw desire.

Lilith's breath faltered.

For one suspended heartbeat, it seemed she would close the distance.

Instead, she withdrew as if burned.

The absence of her touch felt sharper than contact.

"I will not be your rebellion," Lilith said, the softness gone from her voice. "Nor your mere curiosity."

Eve reached instinctively, but Lilith had already stepped back.

Composure reclaimed. Distance restored. She refused to submit out of jealousy and desire. She was desperate to retake power of her own feelings.

"You must decide who you are before you expect me to know you fully," Lilith continued. "I will not be a lesson you return from."

And then she turned away. "Well, what would you like to do in the little time we have?" She said, sounding unaffected. As if nothing had happened.

Eve stood in the fading light, heart pounding, lips still tingling where they had nearly been claimed. And how much she wanted that.

The garden felt charged with something that could no longer be mistaken. And Eve needed to breathe new air before she insisted on finishing what they started.

Lilith did not answer immediately when Eve asked.

"Show me what lies beyond," she had said, the words trembling between impulse and curiosity.

For a long moment Lilith studied her, as if measuring how much knowing Eve could bear.

"You may not wish to see it," Lilith said at last.

"I do."

The edge of Eden was not a wall. Lilith had told her that much before. There was something outside of Eden, and Lilith had been there. She could come and go freely.

Lilith looked into Eve's eyes as she contemplated a moment. Then she smiled. "Alright, but you'll have to do what I say." Eve nodded in agreement.

Without hesitation, Lilith closed the distance between them again, took Eve in her arms. One hand on the small of her back, the other cradled the back of her head. Lilith's fingers tangled in Eve's curls, holding her in place, pressed against her and looking into each other's eyes. Eve held her breath.

"Close your eyes." Lilith instructed. Eve reluctantly obeyed.

In the darkness, she felt warm velvet lips touch her own. Gently first, then firmer. Those lips began to move, coaxing Eve's lips to join the dance. When their lips opened slightly so a small breath could escape. Lilith's tongue slithered between those lips and met Eve's own. They continued kissing like this for what felt like minutes. Lilith's grip tightening in her hair and pulling her closer at the waist. Until Lilith's lips began to slow, and she slowly loosened her hold. And then all at once she pulled back, releasing her and leaving a step between them.

Eve's eyes flew open and her gaze burned into Lilith's, both breathing ragged.

Eve was so lost in what had just happened, in what se was still feeling from it, she didn't notice right away.

Green had surrendered slowly to dust. Grass had turned to brittle stalks. The air lost its sweetness first. Then it's moisture. The sky seemed wider somehow harsher, less forgiving.

Eve slowly turned around where she stood.

The soil beneath her feet was coarse and hot. Pebbles cut at her soles. Wind moved without fragrance. It carried grit instead of pollen.

The land opened into something vast and colorless, ochre and ash and pale, cracked earth stretching toward distant, jagged hills.

Nothing bloomed.

Nothing shimmered.

The sun felt heavier here.

"This is where you have been?" she asked.

"At times."

A flicker of motion caught Eve's attention, something darting low across the ground.

She gasped and stepped closer.

Small flies lifted from the carcass of some long-dead animal, their bodies glinting in the sun as they swarmed and settled again.

"There is life outside of Eden?!" Eve whispered.

Lilith walked up behind her.

"Not without struggle."

Eve crouched, watching the insects move with relentless purpose. There were no blossoms here, no ripe fruit waiting to be plucked. The flies fed on what had fallen.

"They survive on so little," Eve said.

"Yes."

The wind rose, tugging at her hair. In the distance she could see sparse shrubs clinging to life, their roots exposed by erosion.

"How does anything grow?"

"With labor," Lilith answered. "With struggle. They tear from the earth what Eden offers freely."

"They?" Eve's voice trembled.

Lilith's gaze remained fixed on the horizon.

"There are others."

Eve's head snapped toward her. "Others like us?"

"Yes."

The word fell like a stone.

"They build shelters from mud and straw. They till soil that resists them. They bleed for harvest. They bear children who grow, and age. Their backs bend.

Their hands harden. Their teeth fall. Their hair pales. Their skin loosens. And they die."

Eve listened in horror.

"They die?" she asked.

"They die. No forbidden fruit, just disease, time."

The wind did not soften the word.

Eve's throat tightened. "But we don't age."

"In Eden, time is different," Lilith said quietly. "It lingers. Nothing decays. Nothing withers. The fruit ripens but does not rot. Flesh does not sag."

Lilith turned, sweeping her eyes across the barren stretch. That is why this world looked older than Eden.

"Eventually everything here dies," Lilith continued. "Even stone erodes. Even rivers dry."

A strange sound left Eve's chest, something between fear and awe.

"Why?" she demanded. "Why would it be made this way?"

Lilith's expression shifted, not bitter, not angry. Wondering.

"I have walked this land for years. I have asked that question of wind and sand and silence. I have found that when one seeks knowledge, it answers. Though not always kindly."

She knelt and pressed her palm into the cracked earth.

"Creation began with us. But it did not end with us. Perhaps Eden was never meant to contain it."

Eve stared back at Lilith.

"Then what are we meant for?"

Lilith rose slowly.

"Perhaps we are meant to be the image. The model. The first shape of what humanity might become. A catalyst"

"An example?" Eve whispered.

"Yes."

A gust of hot wind struck them full in the face, stinging Eve's eyes. She tasted salt on her lips.

The land did not comfort.

It did not offer.

It demanded.

She imagined hands blistered from digging. Children crying from hunger. Bodies growing thin and old and eventually still.

Her stomach twisted.

"I do not want this," she said faintly.

Lilith stepped closer, not touching.

"Fear not, this is not where you belong."

Eve looked again at the horizon, endless, merciless, alive in a way she had never imagined.

The flies rose again, stubborn, persistent.

Something in Eve fractured, not rebellion this time, but safety.

Her familiar Eden no longer felt like confinement.

It felt like shelter.

She stepped backward without realizing she was doing it.

Lilith noticed her Eve's panic rising. She quickly came to her side "Eve, are you alright?!" She asked urgently, afraid she had given her too much, too soon.

"I want to go back." She said breathlessly.

Lilith's expression shifted, her usual confidence melting into concern, intensity softening into something like fear. She stepped forward, drawing Eve into her arms with a gentleness Eve had not expected. Eve pressed her cheek to Lilith's chest, feeling the steady, ancient rhythm of her heartbeat. She let it calm her.

Lilith lowered her chin to rest atop Eve's head.

"Close your eyes, and think of where you belong," she murmured.

Eve obeyed.

When she could taste the figs in the air again, and the dust dissipated in her throat. Lilith gently released her. "Open your eyes, Eve." She commanded softly.

The green had returned beneath her feet, softness, fragrance, the hum of bees.

The air grew gentle again.

Eve's chest loosened as if she had been drowning.

When she finally looked back to Lilith, Lilith's dark gaze searched hers, worry etched deep.
Eve looked away.

A pit grew in her stomach, heavy, cold, relentless.

*What if she was failing the purpose she had been
created for?*
What if her place had never been hers to choose?

Adam *needed* her.
He had prayed for her.
He had been good to her, steady, warm, proud of her.
He had given her purpose.

Lilith did not *need* her.
Lilith could call forth flowers with a breath, shape life
with desire, summon creation with a word.
Lilith was whole without her.

The thought stung.

Eve lifted her gaze, heart clenched with sudden guilt.

"I have to leave," she whispered. "I must return to
Adam."

As she spoke the words, they felt like betrayal,
betrayal of Lilith, of the awakening inside her,
betrayal even of herself.

For the first time since they met, the surety in Lilith's
eyes fractured.
A shadow of disbelief, then hurt, then something
dangerously close to desperation.

"Why?" Lilith asked softly. "Is that what you truly
want?"

"NO."
The answer burst out before Eve had even realized she was speaking.

Silence fell, heavy as overly ripe fruit.

Eve swallowed hard.

"But it is where I belong," she said, voice small. "He needs me. I came from him… and now I must return."

Lilith stepped closer, the air darkening around her like a storm building behind her skin.

"I was formed from the same clay," she said, her voice low, vibrating with old power. "The same earth. The same sky. The same breath."

She lifted a hand to Eve's cheek, not touching, only hovering close enough that Eve could feel the heat radiating from her skin.
"You were cut from *my* side as much as his."

The words struck Eve like lightning.

Did she truly belong to both? Or could she choose?

The thought ignited a warmth deep in her chest, and lower, a warmth she did not have a name for. She tried to stamp it down.

"He needs me…" Eve said again, though the conviction had drained from her voice.

Lilith's eyes deepened to a shade that felt like
darkness swallowing the last of day.

"And I *want* you."

The words spilled out unguarded, fierce, raw.
Eve's breath caught.

Heat blossomed through her, longing, fear, relief,
desire, tangled so tightly she could no longer tell them
apart.

She stared at Lilith.
For the first time, she saw something fragile flicker
behind Lilith's defiant smile.

A desperate kind of hunger.

Eve turned.

If she stayed a moment longer, she would break or
become something new entirely.
She did not know which frightened her more.

So she walked away.
While she still possessed the strength to do so.

CHAPTER

TWELVE

Eve considered Lilith's words long after the echo faded in her.

What example for humanity was she meant to set?

Adam's purpose felt certain.
He discovered and named the world around them.
Man's understanding took shape beneath his tongue.
He had prayed for a companion, and Eve had been given, bone of his bone, breath of his breath.
He had taught her that she existed because he had asked, and that her purpose was to stand beside him, support him, complete him.

Her chest tightened.

If that was true… then what was she doing with Lilith, in a place shaped by longing, not obedience?

Unease settled inside her.

Though nothing about it felt right anymore, Eve sought comfort in returning to old routines.

She decided she would dedicate herself to setting the best example she could. That she would serve Adam faithfully and take solace in it.

She would seek the company of her animal friends when it wasn't enough. And in time, maybe she too, could *forget Lilith*.

So that's what she tried to do. She would rise with the sun. Forage for food, renewed gratitude for how plentiful it was here. Tend her garden and try not to imagine orchids blooming between Lilith and her when they touched. Feed the bird Adam still kept caged, talk to it though it never talked back. Listen to Adam share his day. Then she would return to Lilith in her sleep, in dreams she had no power over.

The river ran stronger here, narrowed by stone, its surface broken into silver muscle and foam.

Eve had come to the bank alone, drawn by the sound, not the soft lapping she knew from Eden's gentler streams, but something insistent. Urgent.

The fox was already there when she arrived.

It lay stretched across the grass, tail flicking lazily, green eyes tracking the current.

"You hear it," the fox said without looking at her.

"Yes."

"Good."

Eve stepped closer to the edge and saw them, sleek bodies flashing beneath the surface. Salmon. Dozens of them. They surged forward, only to be shoved back by the force of water. Again and again, they hurled themselves upstream, silver flanks catching light before vanishing beneath the churn.

"They will not make it," Eve said instinctively.

Some struck stone and recoiled. Some disappeared into deeper pockets. A few broke through the narrowest passage and vanished into calmer water beyond.

"They are foolish," she added softly. "The river pushes them the other way."

The fox yawned. "So does comfort."

Eve watched one salmon leap, a desperate arc of muscle and will, only to fall short and slam back into the torrent.

She flinched.

"Why don't they turn around?" she asked.

"Because what they seek is not behind them."

The fox rose then, padding lightly to stand beside her. Its shoulder brushed her calf, deliberate but fleeting.

"They were born downstream," it continued. "They feed downstream. They grow strong downstream. But they do not become what they are meant to become there."

Another fish launched itself upward, clearing the stone this time, body trembling as it landed in quieter flow beyond.

Eve's breath caught.

"They choose this?" she whispered.

"They know what they are and how to be that, they didn't have a say in the struggle along the way, they choose to trust it will get calmer if they make it through."

The river roared.

Eve imagined the forked paths. The left one Adam favored, no resistance. Only comfort. And predictable destinations. The one to the right, that Eve had heard calling her, full of obstacles, and requiring trust.

The current before her did not promise safety.
It promised resistance.

One salmon faltered near the edge, exhausted, drifting sideways before gathering itself again.

Eve's chest tightened.

"It would be easier to remain," she said. "To float."

The fox's tail curled around its paws.

"Aye, it would be easier, though it would not be a salmon." The fox teased.

Another leap. Another failure. Another attempt.

Eve's gaze fixed on one smaller salmon that seemed absurdly determined. It leapt, failed, vanished, reappeared, and leapt again.

Her pulse began to match the rhythm of their struggle.

"I am afraid," she admitted.

"Of what?" the fox asked.

"Of swimming against the current."

The fox tilted its head.

"As afraid of swimming in circles fighting the urge to?"

Eve swallowed.

Behind her, Eden remained lush and unmoving. Before her, water carved stone.

The salmon were not rebelling against the river.

They were finding their way in it.

"Does the river ever change its course?" she asked.

"Eventually," the fox replied. "Everything does."

Another fish cleared the final rise.

Eve felt something shift in her chest, not certainty, but possibility.

Perhaps resistance was not proof of error.

Perhaps difficulty was not warning but direction.

The fox stepped away, already losing interest.

"You will swim," it said casually over its shoulder. "Or you will not. The river does not beg."

Eve remained at the bank long after the fox disappeared into the tall grass.

She did not step into the current.

Not yet.

But for the first time, she no longer mistook still water for safety.

Eve made it back to the willows before Adam. She had brought some small seeds for her caged friend.

She went to where the cage sat and laid the seeds just within the branches. But the finch made no move for the food. It perched and did nothing. Despondent, and done flying back and forth with nowhere to go.

Eve felt its pain though it would not ask to be let out. It should not have to ask for freedom.

She couldn't take it anymore. She tore at the vines securing the branches until several gave way. The finch did not hesitate to escape and was gone as fast as it's wings would carry it.

She imagined following it to freedom. But she was not convinced her future lay outside her cage.

For she had now seen what lay beyond paradise, the barren, aching truth of a world without god's breath on its neck. If she wished to remain as she always had in garden, she would need to do what she had always done.

Play the role she was created to play.

Eve understood roles better than she understood freedom.

She looked back down to the ruined cage before her. She knew she should be concerned Adam would be upset. But she couldn't bring herself to feel anything but relief.

When Adam returned, she sought to distract him with pleasure. It worked, as he didn't seem to care at all for their captive, trusting it had what it needed without checking.

She used her body to make him happy like it was reflex, and she tried to find her happiness in his. She tried desperately to feel him slide in and out of her, and be consumed by it. But any arousal she managed to glean was short lived and shallow.

She would wait until Adam slumbered and then roll to the side. She would remember Lilith's hand on the hollow between her thighs after she touched herself, the way she was beginning to now. She thought of Lilith's lips and tongue dancing with hers as her finger danced around the spot that brought her to her pinnacle.

After she rode a single wave of climax at her own hand, she drifted to sleep. Knowing well who she would find there.

She stood once more in Lilith's garden. Eve saw Lilith standing there looking forlorn.

Eve reached out.
"Are you still waiting for me?" she whispered.
"Wanting for me?"

The sky above them split open, darkness swallowing the stars, veins of light tearing through the air like cracks in the firmament. A thunderous sound followed, sharp and violent. Water spilled from the heavens like grief made liquid.

The waking world trembled in answer. Lightning split the sky.

Eve jolted awake as cold water struck her skin.

She gasped. The sleeping grove was drenched. Adam sat up beside her, sputtering, eyes wide with terrified confusion. The sky above them loomed dark, roiling with clouds she had never seen before.

A deafening crack tore across the heavens.

"What is happening?" Adam cried.

Water poured in sheets around them, soaking the earth, battering the leaves, drumming against their skin. Eve felt it vibrate through her bones with the memory of her dream.

Adam grabbed her hand and pulled her toward a nearby alcove of rocks. They stumbled into the shelter as the storm raged, wind yowling like a wounded beast.

"God must be angry with us," Adam said, breathless

and urgent. "He seeks to remind us of his *reign*."

But Eve knew better.

She pressed a trembling hand to her chest, feeling her heartbeat in time with the storm outside.

Adam feared divine wrath.

Eve recognized longing when she saw it.

The sky did not weep because God was angry.

It wept because **Lilith** did.

CHAPTER

THIRTEEN

After the *rain,* as Adam named it, subsided. They attempted to return to normal.

Eve was able to blame the destroyed cage on the angry winds. Lies now coming too easily for her.

She assured him he did not have to rebuild her gift, and encouraged him to venture out and see what damage the storm had done. As she would check on the animals.

Really, she just needed space. She wandered aimlessly.

Eve found the raven at the edge of the orchard where the trees thinned and the sky widened. Fruit littered the floor from the rains.

Adam's voice carried faintly behind her; steady, rhythmic, cataloguing the same branches he had walked a hundred times before. The cadence of certainty. The comfort of repetition.

She did not turn back.

The raven sat upon a low, crooked limb, its feathers absorbing the light rather than reflecting it. One black wing was slightly lifted, mid-preen.

"You don't belong here," Eve said. Ravens were of Lilith's garden.

"Neither do you," the raven answered, voice dry as bark.

Eve stepped closer, unsettled by the way its eye seemed too knowing.

"Why not?"

"You are changing."

The word tightened her chest.

"I have always been the same."

The raven dipped its beak into its wing and tugged loose a long, dark feather. It drifted to the ground between them.

"Have you?"

Eve bent to pick it up. The feather was light. Perfect. Whole.

"You lost it," she said.

"I did."

"Does that not trouble you?"

The raven tilted its head. "Why would it?"

"It was part of you."

"And now it is not."

Eve frowned. "Then you are less."

The raven laughed, a low, rasping sound.

"Feathers fall. They grow again. The sky does not mourn them."

The wind lifted another loose plume from the bird's body, carrying it in a lazy spiral before dropping it at Eve's feet.

"You are falling apart," Eve whispered.

"I am becoming."

The words struck deeper than she expected.

Behind her, Adam called the name of some flowering vine for the third time that week. His voice never changed when he said it. The vine never answered differently.

The raven hopped lower on the branch, close enough that Eve could see the new growth beneath its older feathers; smaller, sharper, still forming.

"You fear loss," it said.

"Yes."

"You mistake it for ending."

Eve's hands tightened around the fallen feather.

"If I venture where I feel pulled," she said slowly, "I may not recognize myself after."

The raven regarded her without sympathy.

"Recognition is a habit," it replied. "evolving is a necessity."

The wind shifted again, warm from the orchard, cooler from the open land beyond.

"Do you regret the feathers you leave behind?" Eve asked.

"They served," the raven said. "Then they were gone."

It stretched both wings wide; uneven, molting, imperfect, yet strong.

"I do not cling to what has finished its purpose." The raven said.

Eve's gaze drifted back toward the garden's center where Adam moved in predictable paths. Safe. Certain. Known.

Lilith was not safe.
Lilith was not certain.

Lilith was the storm.

"And if I fall?" Eve asked quietly.

The raven's eye flashed.

"Everything falls," it said. "Not everything flies."

Eve let the feather slip from her hand.

It did not shatter when it struck the earth.
It did not cry out.
It simply settled.

The raven resumed preening, unconcerned.

Eve stood between the orchard and the open sky,
pulse steadying.

Change no longer felt like betrayal.

It felt like inevitability.

She was not being lured.

She was molting.

And somewhere beyond certainty, something within
her was already growing in.

"Shall we go home." Eve asked, deciding to let
herself evolve.

CHAPTER

FOURTEEN

This welcome was not gentle.

Lilith's hands were warm against Eve's waist as she pulled her in. One hand firm at the small of her back, the other tangling into Eve's loose mane of curls. As if preparing to drop the world out from under her again. She gripped with a soft authority, tilting Eve's head back just enough to claim her mouth.

The kiss was consuming, a rush of breath and warmth and recognition.

Lilith's lips were insistent.
Her mouth was hungry.
Her presence was a storm Eve walked willingly into.

Eve felt herself unraveling, heart pounding in a rhythm older than Eden. Lilith's fingers tightened in her hair, tugging her head back with a rough control that sent a jolt of heat through Eve's spine, not fear, but exhilaration.

"If you are coming back to me," Lilith murmured against her mouth, voice low and dangerous, "then it must be to offer more than a taste."

Her breath ghosted over Eve's lips, warm, claiming, electric.

And Eve did.

Lilith swept Eve into her arms. A hunger growing between the two women. Eve felt herself empowered by the desire building within her.

Lilith felt Eve's hands on her back, moving slowly lower, to run down and end on the curve of her bottom, which she lightly squeezed while kissing her deeper.

Lilith's arms wrapped around Eve acting as an anchor to hold onto in the maelstrom of emotions and sensations that were unlike anything either of them had known before.

"Hands back." Lilith commanded. "I'm going to show you a world you've never seen before. At any time, you can say 'stop', and I'll do so immediately. Otherwise, I'll open your eyes to a new world of possibilities."

Eve's hands moved away, and she realized that Lilith now had free reign to do as she wished, and it suited her well. Unless Eve told her to stop, that is.

Lilith trailed her fingers slowly down Eve's quivering stomach, until they reached her aching core. But the fingers didn't stop there; they slipped inside, to a part of Eve's anatomy she hadn't even been aware of. Like a pressure point for pleasure that lived deep within her, but Lilith knew right where to find it.

"No!" blurted Eve.

Lilith's hand froze where it was, which was somehow more torturous. "Do you want me to stop?"

"No, I want.. I'm not sure, I don't think
I ever want you to stop. But I don't know if I can take it." Eve admitted.

She felt a kiss on her neck. And Lilith felt the resulting clench around her fingers, as Eve moaned softly. Lilith asked, "Shall we find out?"

Eve tilted her head to give Lilith's lips better access to her neck. "How do you know my body so deeply, when we are still so new to each other?"

Lilith's hand moved up to cup Eve's supple breast through, swiping a thumb across the hard peak. It elicited a gasp of surprise and pleasure.

"I know it like I know my own."

Her tongue traced Eve's jugular.

"But I want to know more."

Afterward, Eve lay draped across Lilith's body, her cheek resting over the steady beat of Lilith's heart. She had rested in this position a hundred times with Adam, but nothing about this felt the same. Besides the practical differences, the most notable difference for Eve was how it made her feel.

When she had given Adam pleasure, she felt intrigue at the way she could make him respond to her touch. She felt pride in the powerful feeling of being the source of his pleasure. Even when she managed to feel physical pleasure when he brushed against her clit or suckled her nipples, it felt fleeting, like it was a spark let loose in a damp dwelling. Reminding you only that fire was a possibility, but knowing it would never fully burn there.

With Lilith, every touch scorched a lingering trail along her skin. The nerves at the back of her neck would prickle with each loaded look, and that prickle ran down her spine when Lilith kissed her. Eve knew she could not stand to lose this feeling.

When Adam held her, she felt safe.
She felt cherished.
Sometimes she even felt useful.

But with Lilith…

With Lilith, she felt alive. She felt whole

Lilith traced lazy circles across Eve's back with the back of her fingers, a touch that left a warm trail dancing along her skin. Eve's breaths came soft and uneven; her senses heightened even in stillness. Every glance from Lilith still made her spine prickle, every brush of skin still made her pulse race.

She had felt sparks with Adam, brief moments of possibility.
With Lilith, the sparks became flame, and the flame became something holy.

Eve closed her eyes tightly, willing her heartbeat to slow.

She could not lose this.
She could not lose *her.*

Here, Eve was not named.
She was *known.*

Eve now knew things. Like, once awakened, a soul cannot go back to sleep.

The earlier storm had not asked permission.

It tore through Lilith's garden the same as the rest of Eden, a mess of her own making. Rain heavy as fists, wind bending young stems until they snapped. The carefully layered bed of soil had collapsed, stones dislodged, seedlings half-buried in mud.

Lilith stood in the wreckage, jaw tight.

The storm did not anger her.

Her loss of control did.

She stepped into the ruined terrace without hesitation, bare feet sinking deep into the soaked earth. With efficient movements she began lifting loosened stones, resetting them into place, packing soil back against the retaining wall. Her hands worked quickly.

Eve found her there.

For a moment she only watched, the tension in Lilith's shoulders, the way she moved as though exercising physical control of the collapsing slope might undo the lapse in emotional control. Clearly still innerved by letting her sadness take a toll on the garden.

"You should wait for the ground to settle," Eve said gently.

"I do not wait for what I can mend."

Lilith heaved a larger stone into place, mud splashing up her arms.

Eve stepped down into the terrace without another word.

The earth swallowed her ankles immediately. She nearly slipped.

Lilith glanced back. "Leave it. I will finish."

Eve bent and picked up a fallen stone. "No."

The firmness of the word caught Lilith off guard.

Lilith stared at her for a moment and then smiled to herself. Seeing Eve was determined to work with her, if that's what she needed to do.

Their fingers sank into mud together.

Eve did not rush.
Did not complain.

They worked side by side then hauling stones, lifting sagging edges of earth, reinforcing the terrace wall. Mud streaked Eve's cheek. Damp curls clung to her temples. She slipped once, catching herself against Lilith's shoulder without embarrassment.

Lilith felt the impact, light, unguarded.

Eve laughed at herself and kept working.

She did not expect Eden to right itself.
She did not expect Lilith to shield her from the weight.

She leaned into the labor.

When Eve struggled to lift a heavier rock, Lilith moved to take it.

"Let me."

Eve looked up, breath quick but steady. "No. Together."

Lilith's eyes held hers for a long moment.

Then she adjusted her grip.

They lifted it as one.

Lilith didn't need help. She had proved that in the decades she spent alone. But she accepted it anyway.

Shoulders brushing. Hands muddy. Breath shared in effort.

Something loosened in Lilith's chest.

By the time the final stone was pressed into place, the terrace stood firm again. The seedlings upright. The soil packed tight.

They were covered in mud.

Eve sat back first, pushing wet hair from her face. She looked down at herself and began to laugh, bright and unrestrained.

Lilith stared at her for a heartbeat.

Then, unexpectedly, she laughed too.

Not controlled.
Not measured.
Full.

They walked together toward the waterfall pool, the path slick beneath their feet. The water roared clear and constant.

They stepped in slowly.

Cool water climbed their legs. Mud began dissolving in cloudy ribbons around them.

Eve stood waist-deep, watching Lilith wade ahead toward the waterfall.

Eve approached through the rippling water.

Without thinking, or perhaps thinking very clearly, she lifted her hand and brushed her fingers across Lilith's cheek, wiping away a streak of dried mud.

The touch was gentle.

Lilith stilled.

The old instinct rose, to step back, to deflect, to regain ground.

But Eve's gaze held no presumption.

Only care.

Lilith allowed it.

Then she turned around, so Eve wouldn't see the disarmed look on her face.

When she peeked back over her shoulder, she wore a sly smile. "Will you wash my back?"

The waterfall thundered on, indifferent and constant, as something quieter reshaped itself between them.

Eve regarded Lilith carefully, savoring the sight. Aroused at her request.

The gentle breeze caressed everything above the water, her naked belly, and breast, and her nipples hardened even more. It's a good thing Lilith wasn't looking at her.

Eve silently came up behind her. "Ready?" She asked.

Lilith nodded. Eve began rubbing her hands through the caked dirt turning mud on Lilith's back, feeling the grit against her soft skin beneath.

Eve couldn't help but stare. Mesmerized by the water spilling from her hands and sliding down her back, clearing any dirt, as it touched every inch of her. Eve was jealous of that water.

Lilith suddenly turned, so she was now facing Eve, and Eve's hands slid across the slick flesh at the top of Lilith's full breasts.

"Thank you," Lilith said, while staring directly into Eve's eyes. Heat surged up her chest, neck, and face as the feeling of exposed nerves rose to the surface.

"You know, when you take one of the senses away, the others become more intense," Lilith said, grinning with mischief.

"Close your eyes, Eve."

Eve obeyed. When her world went dark, she felt Lilith gently pull her forward to where the waterfall grew louder. Anticipation swelled in her, then she felt the force of water cascade over her, Lilith stopped her where it continued to flow down her back.

She felt the water more intensely now that she couldn't see. Though, it paled in comparison to the sensation of Lilith's hands sliding across Eve's skin.

As she washed way any remaining mud on Eve's breasts.

Eve shivered, though the water wasn't cold.

"Are your eyes still closed?" Lilith asked, her words barely a whisper.

"Yes."

Eve felt Lilith's hands leave her body once she answered, and she wanted to protest their absence.

But then she felt Lilith's tongue slide over her nipple. Eve gasped. Lilith continued to lap at Eve's nipple, and then the other. Eve unintentionally arched her back, so her chest sprung forward. Lilith greedily took one of Eve's nipples into her mouth and suckled on it.

Eve groaned in appreciation.

Lilith's hand moved lower, and Eve's heart drummed like crazy as she trailed a circle around her navel. Eve could hardly breathe.

Eve felt water swirl around them, and then she felt the heat of Lilith's body press against hers. The hardened peaks of their breasts now rubbing against one another with the slightest movement.

Lilith's breath was on her lips, and before she knew it, she was kissing her. Soft and sweet.

Fire surged through Eve's body, her face in Lilith's hands, letting her tongue part her lips and deepen the kiss. She tasted like the sweetest fruit, and Eve couldn't get enough of her soft lips and skillful tongue.

Eve wanted it everywhere.

Lilith wrapped her hands around Eve's waist, pulling her in closer to her.

Eve didn't stop her when her fingers slipped under the water, teasing beneath the dark curls that moved in rhythm with the water and sending spikes of pleasure between her legs. Her deft finger finding the spot Eve didn't have a name for with ease. That small pearl at the top of her oyster.

Eve's eyes flew open then. She looked in shock at Lilith. "Please, that spot." She begged, a plea for what she wasn't sure.

Lilith smiled wickedly. "Clitoris."

Eve's clitoris twitched as if answering to its name, or to Lilith's coaxing finger.

"Adam never taught me that name." Eve said. Still in awe of finally being discovered.

"That doesn't surprise me." Lilith said almost in jest.

Eve then lost her train of thought as Lilith's finger began small circles, causing Eve's pleasure to build.

Her other hand fondling Eve's breast.

Eve bit her bottom lip.

Suddenly Lilith slid down dipping beneath the water until she was fully submerged. Eve looked down shocked, and missing Lilith's hands and mouth on her.

Then as if in answered prayer. Lilith's mouth found her again.

This time lapping and suckling at that swollen aroused pearl. Eve couldn't see her well beneath the water, but she felt every languid move of her tongue.

Eve was her bursting; she felt wave after wave of pleasure building. Ready to topple over the edge.

She probably should have been worried that Lilith may drown to bring her to the precipice, or more so that right now she wasn't sure she cared. Cause she had reached her climax.

Loud moans, barely drowned in the sounds of the waterfall, filled the air. Lilith waited to feel every rhythmic throb of Eve's orgasm, before finally coming up for air.

CHAPTER

FIFTEEN

Lilith worked among the thorned vines that bordered the outer edge of her garden.

The plant required shaping, not taming, she would insist, but guiding. Its branches had grown wild after the storm, lashing into one another, strangling new growth beneath older, hardened stems.

She worked with practiced precision.

One branch resisted.

She pressed harder.

The thorn pierced her palm before she felt it. A thin line of red welled instantly against her skin.

Lilith did not flinch.

She withdrew the thorn without comment and reached for the next branch.

"Stop."

Eve's voice carried from behind her.

Lilith froze, confused.

A hand closed firmly around her wrist.

"You are bleeding."

"It is nothing." Lilith assured.

The words were reflex.

Eve turned her hand over despite the resistance, examining the wound with quiet focus. Blood slipped down Lilith's wrist in a narrow line.

"It is not nothing," Eve said.

"It will heal."

Eve did not argue.

She simply began walking toward the river, still holding Lilith's hand.

Lilith could have pulled free. She didn't.

The river ran cool and steady along the grove's edge. Eve knelt at the bank and drew Lilith down beside her.

"Give it to me."

It was not a command.

It was an expectation.

Lilith extended her injured hand.

Eve lowered it into the water carefully. Mud and blood clouded briefly before the current carried them away.

The cut was not deep, but it would scar if left untended.

Eve lifted Lilith's hand into the light, examining it as though it were something rare.

Lilith watched her face.

There was no fear there.

No fragility.

Only intent.

"You think me so fragile?" Lilith asked.

Eve's fingers moved gently, pressing clean water into the wound to rinse it thoroughly.

"The last thing I would call you is fragile," she said. "I simply think you are worth nurturing."

The words cut deeper than the thorn had.

Lilith had never been nurtured. She wouldn't let herself be.

Care had always come with condition.
With hierarchy.
With expectation of obedience.

Eve did not ask permission.

She did not ask Lilith to admit pain.

She simply cared.

Lilith's breath faltered, not from the sting of the cut, but from the unfamiliar weight of being tended without condition.

"I have endured worse," Lilith said quietly.

"I know," Eve replied.

She lifted Lilith's hand to inspect her work, fingers lingering just a moment longer than necessary.

"That does not mean you must endure alone."

Lilith felt something loosen, not pride, not strength, but the belief that accepting gentleness diminished her.

Eve was not asking her to kneel.

She was asking her to allow.

"Done," Eve said.

Lilith looked at her.

"You do not fear that I might need you," Lilith observed.

Eve shook her head once.

"I hope you do."

The simplicity of it undid her more than any grand declaration could have.

Lilith let her injured hand rest in Eve's grasp a moment longer.

The wound throbbed faintly.

But something else inside her quieted.

She had survived alone by hardening.

Eve was teaching her that survival and connection were not enemies.

That yielding to care did not strip her of power.

It reshaped it.

Lilith rose slowly, offering her uninjured hand to help Eve to her feet.

This time, when Eve took it, Lilith did not brace.

She let the contact remain.

Not submission.

Not dominance.

Connection.

And it felt stronger than either.

Lilith found Eve laying back in the tall grass where the orchard thinned toward open sky, one arm folded beneath her head, the other resting loosely at her side.

"You seem very pleased," Eve murmured, looking up at her.

"I brought you something." Lilith said.

She lifted the stem of a pale blossom she had plucked from the thorned vines she had been guiding. It was delicate. Wild. Petals soft as breath.

Lilith's gaze sharpened slightly. Then she lay beside Eve, propped up on her elbow, so she was over Eve.

"What are you doing?" Eve asked.

"Tending you." Lilith replied.

The flower hovered just above Eve's collarbone before settling there, light enough not to press. Lilith dragged it slowly downward, across the smooth plane of her shoulder, over the curve where strength met grace.

Eve did not move.

Lilith trailed the blossom lower, following the line of curves, then circling back upward instead of continuing.

The petals skimmed the hollow of Eve's throat. Paused. Shifted.

Eve's breath deepened despite herself.

Lilith noticed.

She moved the flower down again, this time along the center of Eve's chest, careful, so careful, never to let her fingers touch where the stem passed. The restraint was its own heat.

Eve's jaw tightened.

"Are you trying to torture me?" she asked, voice low.

Lilith leaned closer. Close enough that her shadow crossed Lilith's face.

"No," she whispered.

The blossom traced the slow line of Eve's ribs, then drifted toward her hip, hovering just above skin before dipping lightly, grazing, retreating again.

Eve's fingers gripped the grass.

"You are cruel," she murmured halfheartedly.

Lilith smiled, soft, not mocking.

"I am patient."

The flower traveled upward again, never lingering long enough to satisfy, never pressing hard enough to claim. Over shoulder. Across collarbone. Along the curve of her neck. Causing small bumps to raise along Eve's skin where ever it went

Eve's eyes had closed now.

Not in surrender.

In concentration.

The petals slipped down once more, this time dipping between Eve's thighs, and sliding along her now wet center.

Eve's eyes opened.

Dark.

Burning.

Lilith stared back into those burning amber eyes, as she slid the flower against Eve.

Collecting her juices like dew upon the petals.

Until it was too much for Eve to bare. Her body arched against the grass, and she began to moan through her orgasm. Lilith covered Eve's mouth with her own, swallowing her moans of ecstasy.

One morning, as they lay tangled in the moss, the air cool, the leaves whispering overhead. Lilith trailed her fingers across Eve's collarbone. The touch was soft, but her gaze was sharp, studying every flicker of emotion on Eve's face.

She had noticed small moments where Eve seemed distant. Or even distraught.

"Are you not happy here with me?" Lilith asked.

Her voice was sincere, not jealous, not accusing. Only searching.

Eve curled closer, pressing her face into the warm hollow between Lilith's shoulder and throat.

"I am happy," she whispered. "I am only unhappy that he does not know. That he cannot see what he would ask me to give up."

Lilith's hand stilled for a moment, only a moment, but Eve felt the subtle change at mention of him.

"He chooses not to see," Lilith said, voice sharpening like flint struck against stone. "Like my purpose, and then my existence, he chooses to ignore what does not serve him."

A small flare of defensiveness sparked in Eve's chest. "He's gentle," she murmured softly. "He provides for me, wants to keep me safe."

Lilith sat up in one fluid, graceful movement. Her hair fell down her back like a cascade of midnight.

"No," she said, and this time her voice held steel. "He wants to *keep* you. There is a difference."

Eve froze. She couldn't help picturing the bird in the cage.

The truth, spoken aloud, cut deeper than she expected.

Lilith held her gaze, unflinching, unashamed.

"For him, you are a prize. Reward. His prayer made flesh. For me,"
She touched Eve's cheek, fingers trembling with a new vulnerability.
"*you are everything.*"

Adam had claimed her body.
Lilith had let Eve claim her soul.

Lilith had submitted to Eve in a way Adam wouldn't even understand.

Eve swallowed, throat aching. "I don't want to hurt him."

Lilith's jaw tightened.
"And what of hurting yourself?"

Silence stretched between them.

Finally, Lilith stood, drawing herself to her full height, beautiful, wild, unbowed.

"I will not share you," she said, not harshly, but with quiet resolve.
"Not with him."

The words slid into Eve's chest like a key and a blade all at once.

Her heart thrashed.

She wanted to answer.
She wanted to say *I choose you.*
She wanted to collapse into Lilith's arms and let the world burn itself quiet.

But something heavy and ancient tugged at her ribs.

Duty.
Purpose.
Fear.

Eve rose unsteadily to her feet.

Lilith's eyes softened in the same moment they sharpened, hope and despair warring behind them.

Eve stepped back.

"I…"
But no words came.

She had decided to come here, she had stayed for weeks and savored Lilith. But she never let herself believe it could go on forever.

She was afraid of Lilith deciding she might one day tire of her and walk away when Eve asked for something she wasn't willing to give.

She knew Adam would never grow bored, never reach for more.

So Eve turned and walked away first.

Lilith did not follow.
But the garden behind Eve trembled as though it wanted to.

CHAPTER

SIXTEEN

Eve followed the familiar path back toward Adam, the forest light soft and unquestioning around her.

Soon she would be folding herself neatly back into the rhythm expected; fruit gathered, questions unasked, her body offered without complication. With him, her place was defined. Named. Secure. He would not leave; safety clung to him like bark to tree. And yet with every step she felt the faint drag of something unseen, as if the earth itself resisted her direction. Safety should not feel like retreat. Belonging should not taste like surrender.

She slowed where paths divided; one curving deeper into the orchard that led back to Adam, the other winding toward a place he would never be.

The air shifted as she neared the tree, thinner,

watchful. Eve told herself she only needed a moment to steady her thoughts. Only to breathe before returning to what was known.

Eden lay in a hush so complete it felt afraid to stir.

The serpent was already waiting. As if called back by her longing for answers.

It coiled at the base of the tree's roots, silver scales glinting faintly with an inner glow. It lifted its head when she approached, tongue flickering once, tasting the air around her.

"You smell of endings," it said.

Eve wrapped her arms around herself.
"I don't know how to tell him," she whispered.

Eve wasn't sure when she had decided. But she was sure as she spoke. She wasn't returning to resume her place with Adam. She was returning to tell him she found her placc with Lilith.

Her voice trembled despite the warm night.
"I don't know how to break something he doesn't believe is already broken."

The serpent slivered betwixt the roots.

"You do not need him to believe it," it murmured. "As long as *you* do."

Eve closed her eyes. Her breath shook. The weight of truth pressed against her ribs like a hand seeking entrance.

She looked up at the forbidden fruit, glowing faintly

on its branches, suspended like captured stars.
Her heart squeezed painfully at the memory of Lilith's touch, her laughter, her fire.

"I feel something different for her," Eve admitted, voice unsteady. "Something more than I have ever felt. She inspires joy and passion in me, but also courage. She makes me feel bold and vulnerable at the same time."

She pressed a hand to her chest, as though to hold it all inside.
"This is not a feeling I have ever known with Adam… and I don't think it's one he has ever known either."

The serpent slid closer until its smooth body brushed the tops of her feet.

"Perhaps it is a feeling only you can name." The serpent said.

There was no name for what she felt for Lilith. There was no name for most feelings in Eden.

Adam named the animals, and the trees, and the flowers, the world around them. But he had never thought to name the world within them.

Though Eve had felt so many things so keenly, she had never tried to name them aloud. Maybe man would always struggle to name such things out loud.

Eve thought about what Lilith had said about them being the model for all that was and all to come. If she continued to feel in secret, to never name these things inside out loud, perhaps she would be dooming more than herself.

She wouldn't be hiding half herself to protect others and protect their peace. She would be denying what they were all capable of when they allowed themselves to feel without fear.

To live in truth.

She would be living a lie with Adam, and she would be withholding a life from Lilith.

She could no longer try to control what Adam would feel about all of this. His feelings were no more her responsibility than hers were his. He did not make her feel this for Lilith by not feeling enough for her.

This is just who she was inside, and she no longer wanted to leave it nameless.

Eve pressed her palm to her sternum, feeling her heartbeat thudding wildly beneath. She exhaled, a sound caught somewhere between a sob, a laugh, and a prayer.

The serpent circled her once, then stilled.

Quietly, softly, trembling with truth.

"I *love* Lilith."

The words broke open something inside her.
Something raw.
Something sacred.
Something that had waited since the dawn of creation to be spoken aloud.

The serpent bowed its head.

Eve wiped her eyes. She did not remember crying.

Her chest throbbed with the ache and the relief of it all.

For the first time since her creation, Eve did not feel small, not secondary, not named.

She felt chosen.
By herself.
By truth.
By love.

Now she only wished to know if Lilith would love her back.

SEVENTEEN

Eve returned to Lilith's garden as dawn softened the
edges of the world.
Her steps were guided less by memory than by the
pull in her chest, a thread tied to her ribs, tugged
gently toward home.

Lilith stood still, hands clasped loosely before her, as
though she had been waiting for Eve for days… or
centuries.

She did not speak.
She did not gasp in surprise. Or fault Eve for leaving.
Her eyes burned with a truth that seemed to see
through Eve's skin, through her ribs, into the quiet
center of her soul.

Eve stepped forward.
Lilith moved at the same time, closing the distance

with a certainty that broke Eve's breath in half.

Her hands slid down Eve's sides as though tracing sacred lines carved into the stone of a temple. Her mouth pressed soft, reverent kisses to Eve's skin, not claiming, not demanding, but worshiping.

Lilith kissed her like someone who knew the shape of her soul, not just her body.

Eve tasted figs and storm winds and something divine.

She could have drowned in that kiss.
She wanted to.

But Eve pulled back with great restraint, cupping Lilith's face in both hands so she could look into her eyes.

"What is this?" she whispered.
Her voice cracked.
Raw. Bare. Unhidden.

Lilith brushed her thumb across Eve's trembling lower lip and smiled, knowingly.

"This," Lilith said gently, "is love."

The word broke something open inside Eve.

Her breath hitched.
Her knees weakened.
Tears, unbidden and unstoppable, spilled down her cheeks.

Lilith caught one on her thumb, her brows knitting in tenderness.

"I have felt it for some time," Lilith confessed, her voice uncharacteristically breathless. "After you walked into my life, into *this* place, I felt it stir inside me like fruit swelling on a branch. I could feel it in my soul, but I could not name it."

She laughed, soft and incredulous.
"Because this feeling did not begin *from* me. It began *with* you."

Eve choked on a sob.

Lilith continued, words tumbling now.
"I could not ask the world for its name, because I think it is something that can only be found with another. But today…" Her smile grew reverent. "The word came to me without warning. Fully formed. Alive. True."

She pressed her forehead to Eve's.
"I love you, Eve."

Eve's tears came harder at that, wild and grateful and overwhelming.

"I named it today," Eve whispered.
Her voice was a tremor of awe.
"I didn't know it was in my power to name."

Lilith lifted Eve's face in her hands, her own eyes glistening.

"Oh, my darling Eve," she breathed, brushing a kiss to her brow, "you have more power than you know."

Eve swallowed thickly, trying to steady her voice.

"When Adam names things," she said, "he tells me

the names, and I remember them. But with you… why did you know 'love' the moment I named it, even though we were apart?"

Lilith considered that, her brows drawing together.

"Perhaps," she said slowly, "it is not something that can be learned by explanation. It must be felt. Fully."

Her smile softened.
"I knew love's name without being told because I had already known it nameless."

Eve beamed, radiant, relieved, undone.
To be loved in return, deeply, openly, defiantly, was a joy she hadn't known a body could hold.

But the joy dimmed quickly.
A shadow passed behind her eyes.

"So Adam still doesn't know?" she whispered.

Lilith's smile vanished instantly, her expression hardening like cooling stone.

"It is not our concern what Adam knows," she snapped.
The word *our* sounded like a shield.
"If you are choosing me, choosing love, then leave him in your past. Forget him, as he forgot me."

Eve's heart clenched.

"I cannot do that," she said quietly.

Lilith's face twisted in confusion, then injury.

"I do not forget the names I learn," Eve continued.
"Or the one's who taught them. I may not feel the

same love for him… but I still feel for him."

Lilith stared at her, jaw tight.

Eve pressed on, voice soft but steady.
"If I had not first known his companionship, his gentleness, his care… I may not have known love was *more* than that when I found it with you. The contrast made it clear."

She swallowed, feeling raw and exposed.

"I needed you both to understand the full shape of myself."

Lilith blinked in shock, wonder flickering through her anger.

"And I don't think he ever truly forgot you," Eve whispered. "There is a doubt in him. A wound. A space where your name should be."

Lilith's breath caught.

Wind rippled through the fig leaves overhead as though the world leaned in to listen.

For a long moment, Lilith said nothing, only stared at Eve with something like awe, admiration, and heartbreak all braided together.

Finally, she exhaled.

"Very well," she said softly.
"My love."

The words landed like a blessing.

"Go to him," Lilith continued, her voice gentler now.

"Try to make him understand. Try to teach him. Perhaps…" She breathed out slowly, carefully. "Perhaps there is a life for us all in Eden, if he can accept our love for what it truly is."

Eve's heart surged with promise at the thought.

"I never hated him," Lilith said, brushing a stray curl behind Eve's ear. "I simply refused to kneel to him."

She cupped Eve's cheek with fierce tenderness.

"Go. Speak truth. But regardless of what he thinks…"
Her thumb stroked Eve's jaw.
"Return to me. Let us make this place of longing into a place of love."

Lilith kissed her then, Deep, slow, certain. The kiss curling through Eve like a vow.
The taste of sweet figs and wild earth.
The heat of breath against breath.
The promise of something greater than any one life could hold.

When Lilith's tongue slithered across Eve's, it reminded her of the serpent coiling at the base of the tree.

Courage unfurled inside Eve like a bloom opening toward sunlight.

And when the sun was high, high enough that shadows fled, high enough that she could look Adam in the eyes without flinching, Eve left the wild garden of longing.

She walked back toward the familiar Eden she and Adam had shared.

But she did not return as the woman she had been.

She returned as someone who had named love.
And been claimed by it in return.

EIGHTEEN

Eve found Adam beneath the olive trees, weaving vines into a crown.

It was something he had often done when they were new to each other, a quiet ritual, a sign of affection. Seeing him do it now, hands steady, brow relaxed, struck her with a strange ache. A different life lived in that memory. A simpler one. A smaller one.

He looked up the moment she approached.

Relief flooded his face.

"Eve," he breathed. "Where have you been? I searched everywhere. I called your name for days. You didn't answer. I feared you lost and searched until I was just forced to wait."
His eyes darted over her features, worried. "Did you take a new path?"

"I did," she said.

The words held far more meaning than he knew.

She knelt before him. Her heart pounded so hard she thought it might burst open through her ribs.

"Adam," she whispered, "I found **her**."

The words landed like stones dropped into deep water, rippling outward.

His hands froze around the half-woven crown.

"…Who?" he asked, though something flickered in his eyes. A shadow of a memory he could not fully grasp.

"*Lilith,*" Eve said. "I found Lilith. And we found more in each other. Something new. Something powerful. I named it love. And I feel it for her."

The vine crown snapped in his hands.

His brows slammed together, his face hardening so fast it frightened her.

"Lilith!" he spat, as if the name itself burned his tongue.
"Lilith?!"

Eve's breath caught. The birds scattered and fled at his disturbance.

He remembered her. As though the speaking of her name unlocked the memories. Too easily unearthed from the shallow grave he had buried them.

"You are mine," Adam snapped, rising sharply to his

feet. "You were made from me, from my bone, *for me.*"

"I am my own," Eve said softly.

Her voice did not waver.

"And even if it were not so," she continued, "your bones give you no more right to me than hers. Was she not formed from the same clay?"

The fire in Adam's eyes roared at that.

The same refusal Lilith had once given him returned now through Eve's mouth. His face twisted. Not with grief. Not with heartbreak.

But with possession.

"You're confused," he growled. "She has twisted you. Poisoned you. That…Devil."

"She is no devil," Eve defended, growing in courage "She only allowed me to see that I was capable of more, that I am more."

That was when Adam struck her.

A sharp crack split the air.

Eve's head snapped to the side.
Heat bloomed across her cheek.
Her hand rose instinctively to cover the sting.

Shock held her still.
She had never known violence.
Not from Adam.
Not from anyone.

Her vision blurred.
Not from pain, but from the sudden collapse of everything she thought she knew.

"More than who?!" Adam shouted.
"More than me?!"

Eve tried to step back, but her legs shook too hard.
She barely shifted before he grabbed her wrist.

"You belong to me!" he snarled, dragging her toward him.

She screamed. Not because it hurt. But because it changed everything. And she was completely lost in a place she no longer felt safe, no longer knew, with a stranger.

She stumbled backward, trying to wrench her arm free.
Her other hand pushed against his chest, the chest she once leaned on, but his strength overwhelmed hers.
He seized both her wrists and shoved them down his body easily, for his strength far outmatched her own.
He only stopped when her hands were on his manhood.

She immediately flexed her wrists back as much as she could, so her hands were touching him as little as she could manage. The thought of being made to touch this man she no longer recognized making her stomach turn.

"This is the only thing your hands should be tending," he hissed in her ear. "No more of that useless garden, and certainly no more of that creature's cunt."

Adam released her wrists then, so suddenly that she stumbled back and to the ground, sick and horrified.

"From now on, you will do only what you were made to." He said glaring down at her.

"N..No." Eve barely got out.

His face was twisted into something she didn't recognize.
Not the man who laughed with her beneath the midday sun.
Not the man who taught her names.
Not the man who prayed for her.

Adam's nostrils flared with rage. He suddenly dropped down above her. Pinning her down. His hands rough. His mouth once gentle, now a weapon. As he took what she would no longer give.

"This," he hissed, pushing her down, "is what you were made for."

The world blurred.
The olive branches shuddered.

Eve's terror rose like a tide.

Her hands were trapped.
Her voice was useless.
Her body was held down by the man who once promised safety.

Something inside her cracked.

A small, sacred thing.

A thing that could not be repaired.

As Adam bared down on her, she thrashed and fought. She prayed to him to stop. But her prayers fell on death ears.

There was no ceremony, no sacrament. This was sacrilege.

She was held down by two stone arms. She fought for breath under the unbearable weight of him. He knocked her thighs apart with the bruising force of his knee. Her head flung side to side in panicked protest, as he thrust himself inside her. Her body attempting to close so tightly, it felt torn open when it failed beneath his force. He grunted an angry satisfied grunt as he buried himself as deep as he could.

Eve stilled, despite the burning sting between her legs, she could no longer scream. No longer fight. No longer pray.

She was a statue, jolted lifelessly with each thrust pounding into her. Tears spilled out the corners of her eyes and into her hair without her even feeling them.

She didn't feel anything anymore.

When it was done, Adam's rage drained from him with his seed.

He rolled off of her, chest heaving, his body slack with the release of something vile he mistook for control.

Eve did not look at him.

She turned her face into the dirt, as if she could plant herself to escape him.

The grass beneath her cheek was damp with her tears.

She began to crawl away on shaking elbows.
Then slowly rose to her hands and knees. Her legs
wobbled and buckled as she tried to stand.
Her stomach churned.

She made it only a few feet before the sickness inside
her surged again.
She retched violently onto the ground.

When there was nothing left inside her, she pushed
herself upright, barely, and staggered to her feet.

She did not look back.

She couldn't bear to see which version of him she
would find looking back.

The trees around them were deathly still.
The wind refused to move.
There were no birds to sing.

Even Eden held its breath.

Eve took one trembling step.
Then another.

She felt blood slide down her thighs.
She looked down, startled by how ashen her skin
looked beneath the red.

For the first time, Eden felt cold. Too cold.

Her mind barely held onto thoughts as she walked.
They flickered, scattered, vanished before she could
grasp them.

The path she had taken was aimless at first. Until she

realized she had been walking towards Lilith.

At first, she wanted to run.
To throw herself into Lilith's arms.
To be held.
To be healed.
To be loved.

But then a new feeling rose in her, *shame*, rose inside her like bile.

Shame of her body, a feeling she had never known before. For the first time she wished she could cover herself.

Her body had become unrecognizable.
Marked.
Tainted.
Filled with the memory of what Adam had done to it, what she let him do.

She couldn't bear the thought of Lilith seeing her like this.
Seeing what remained of her.

Surely Lilith would no longer want her.
Surely love had no place in a body that had been remade into a ruin.

So Eve turned away from the path to Lilith.

She walked toward the one place she had always known could end her.

The Tree of Knowledge of Good and Evil.

Its branches loomed like judgment.
Its trunk rose like a monument.

Its fruit glowed faintly, pulsing like sorrow.

The serpent was not there.
No voice guided her.
No presence tempted her.

Only silence.

Eve reached toward the fruit. Her hand did not
tremble. Her heart barely beat.

She plucked the fruit without ritual, without
hesitation, without fear.

She bit into it.

It tasted like ash and honey.
Like endings and beginnings.

She swallowed.

Then she lay beneath the tree, curling her bruised
body into its roots.

She pressed her cheek to the earth.

"Let it end," she prayed.
"Let me be unmade."

And Eve closed her eyes.

NINETEEN

Adam knelt in the grove where he and Eve had spent most of there nights together, since her first breath.

Thc willow branches that had once sheltered their laughter, their rest, their shared warmth, now felt foreign. As if Eden itself had tilted away from him.

The ground beneath him was still soft with the imprint of her body.
He could see it even when he closed his eyes.
Eve walking away from him
The bruises on her skin. The marks he had put there, had bloomed so quickly.
Her eyes had dimmed.
And she had walked away from him without looking back.

At first he thought he should run to her.

Apologize.
Fall to the earth and beg forgiveness.
Swear never again.

But something else, darker, nameless at first, had
rooted itself in the hollow left by her absence.
It pinned him where he was.

A feeling he had no name for.

Then, slowly, painfully, the word formed in his mind.

Shame.

The knowledge of it struck him so violently he
clutched at his chest.

The trees around the grove seemed to pull back,
shuddering away from him.
Leaves rustled in recoil.

And into that thick, suffocating hush, came the voice.

The voice Adam had not heard since his making.

"**Adam**." Came the voice of God.

The ground trembled beneath him.

He collapsed fully now, hands splayed in the earth,
forehead pressed to the soil that no longer felt warm.

"My Lord," Adam gasped, tears spilling until they
soaked the ground.

God's voice, once a comfort, once the echo of
creation itself, was not gentle this time.

It was a storm contained inside a single word.

Adam's whole body shook.
He pressed himself lower, trying to sink into the dirt.

"I..I have done wrong," he stammered, though the words tasted like ashes.
He wasn't sure whether he said them to repent or to escape the weight crushing his chest.

"You have committed a great evil," God said, the tone thunderous and devastating.
"The first mortal sin."

Adam's breath caught.
"No! No, Eve. *Eve made me*. She defied me! She betrayed me with *her*," he spat, hatred curling his voice. "She drove me to it!"

"Enough."

The word rippled outward, trees bending, wind rolling away from the grove like a wave.

"You harmed her," God said, voice heavy with a sorrow Adam had no name for.
"You silenced her. You forced her body to obey yours."

Adam tried to speak, but his throat closed.

"You used violence, oppression, violation," God continued, "where there should have been choice."

Adam choked out a sob, not from remorse, but fear.

God's voice rose, not with volume, but with grief sharpened to a blade.

"You believed she was yours to claim. Yours to touch.

Yours to break."

"She was made for me!" Adam cried.

God thundered then, shaking the grove to its roots.

"She was never yours."

The words struck Adam so forcefully he fell
backward, catching himself with scraped palms.

"Eve belongs only to herself," God said.
"As all of my children do."

Adam shook his head violently.
"No, no, she... she turned from me. She turned to
Lilith." Her name tasted like poison in his mouth.

"Yes," God said.
"And she turned toward her freely, of her own free
will."

Adam's stomach knotted.

"No. No, she was meant for me," he whispered again
like a psalm, voice cracking. "I asked for her. I prayed
for her."

"You prayed for a companion who would know you
and respect you for what you are," God said.
"And *now* she does."

Adam felt his insides twist.
He squeezed his eyes shut as though the truth itself
burned.

"I was afraid," he whispered.
"She, she changed. She slipped away from me. She
wanted more than me."

"She wanted more *for* you," God corrected sharply. "And you refused to grow into the man this garden, this world needed."

Adam stared numbly at the ground.

"Lilith," he muttered, trembling. "She ruined everything. She poisoned Eve against me."

"Lilith ruined nothing," God said sharply. "She acted in accordance with the gift I gave all mankind, free will, she chose truth and knowledge over submission."

Adam flinched at the words.

"She stood beside you as an equal, and you feared her strength," God said. "Eve loved you gently, and you feared losing her. You used fear to justify cruelty, violence, sin." "Sin you chose. And when you did," God said quietly, "She defiled her choice."

Adam blinked, bewildered, angry. "She should have *chosen* ME. Not Lilith, another who rebelled against me!"

"Lilith could not rebel against you, you are not her god." God stormed.

"She did not rebel against me, she honored the gift I gave her when she chose a life apart from the clear one before her." God said, "As did Eve, when she let herself fall, *not from grace*, but in love."

"Her choice was never you or Lilith. Her choice was the one I had been waiting to see someone make. And when your assault shattered her spirit, she went to the tree and finally made full use of my gift."

Adam gasped. "Eve ate the fruit?" His grief for her was quickly replaced by his confusion and something like hope. "Then it was *her* who committed the sin!"

"**No!**" God's booming voice knocked Adam on his back. "She fully embraced free will. Lilith began the journey all that time ago, but she has built her life still within the bounds of the limit I set. As much as she reaches for knowledge, she still never dared eat from the one forbidden tree that promised it. Not because she didn't want to, but because I said she shall not and she was still bound by the choice I made for her. And is it really free will if it is limits?" God asked, "Eve took it further, and broke free of those limits. She chose right, when she knew wrong would be easier. That is the beauty of choice, it is not choosing to do what is right when it is the easy choice or when wrong is simply not an option. It is choosing to take a hard path that you feel is truly worth walking." God said with a touch of something else ringing through.

Pride.

"You wanted us to die?!" Adam asked bewildered.

"Eve is not dead, Adam."

There was a small weight that lifted from Adam's soul then. "But she ate from the forbidden fruit." Adam stated. "You told Lilith and I that the fruit would surely kill us."

"Without a command to break," God said, "how could humanity learn the full power of choice? The ultimate choice only Eve was powerful enough to make."

Adam stared, unable to comprehend.

"Eve was given the choice, and she did not choose death," God continued, voice resonant.
"She *chose life*, a life with knowledge, with pain, with endless possibility."

Adam felt everything inside him rupture.

He wanted to scream.
He wanted to tear the world apart with his bare hands.
He wanted to drag Eve back and chain her to the life he had imagined for them.

But mostly, painfully, he wanted to understand.

He whispered, barely audible,
"Where is she now?"

"On her way to Lilith," God said.

Adam could not tell whether it was grief or rage he felt.

"You, Adam," He said, "chose to use your free will to take another's. To desecrate my greatest gift."

"For that," God said,
"you are **cast out**."

Adam collapsed forward, fingers clawing into the dirt.
"No, please, no. I can change! I can learn…"

"You can," God said, "But not here.
Not in the place you defiled."

Adam sobbed so violently the trees shook with him.

"But what of Eve?" he begged.

"She may remain," God said.
"She will heal. She will grow the garden beyond what
it was."

Adam coughed on another sob.
"And she… she will forget me?"

"No," God said.
"No, Adam. She will not forget. No woman will
forget what they now know man is capable of."

Adam broke then.
Truly broke.
He crumpled onto his side, clutching himself.

The air stilled.
The trees straightened.

And Adam was alone.

Completely, utterly alone.

A man grieving the loss of everything
he had destroyed
with his own hands.

CHAPTER

TWENTY

Eve awoke beneath the Tree of Knowledge with her cheek pressed to it's roots.

At first she didn't breathe. Didn't blink. Didn't dare move.

She had expected oblivion, the soft-bellied nothingness she imagined death must be, and instead she opened her eyes to find the world staring back at her.

The leaves above her glowed with a haze of light, trembling like they were weeping.
The sky was painfully blue.
The earth was warm where her body had lain.

And she, shattered, blood-stained, ruined in ways she had no language for, was still alive.

Her brows knit together, confusion tugging at her

features.

A tremor moved through her chest.
Not anger.
Not grief.

Something quieter.
Stranger.

Relief.

Just a drop, a moment of salve on her soul.

The world looked unchanged, but everything *felt different*.

Sharper.
Heavier.
Clearer.

The scent of soil, moss, crushed leaves made tears spill down her cheeks without warning.

The colors around her seemed to vibrate. Eden felt deeper than before. And farther away.

She touched her own arm, fingertips grazing a bruise forming along her bicep.
She flinched, but the pain no longer swallowed her whole.
It was simply there, a testament.

Her heart's bruises were rawer.
Exposed.
Bleeding in ways the body could not show.

She drew a shuddering breath.

"I am still here," she whispered to herself.

A soft, familiar hiss broke the silence.

"Yessss. You are."

The serpent appeared above her, and coiled gracefully around one of the tree's branches, lowering its head until its golden eyes matched her line of sight.

"But You don't have to be," it added.

Her breath caught.
"What do you mean?"

"You may still die," the serpent said simply.
"If that is your will."

No deception.
No coaxing.
Just a truth laid bare before her.

She swallowed.

"But first," the serpent continued, "you should know something."

Eve's voice wavered.
"What do you wish me to know?"

"That choosing death *will* end your suffering," it said
"Your pain. Your shame. Your fear." The serpent continued, to Eve's surprise. She expected to be persuaded otherwise.

Its gaze softened, uncoiling slightly.
"*But* it will also end your joy. Your pleasure. Your capacity for love."

That last word cut through her like a blade.

Love.

Eve closed her eyes.

Love was the feeling she had named.
Love was the heat of Lilith's hands on her skin.
Love was the ache beyond her ribs when Lilith looked
at her like she was something worth knowing.

But now…
Now she felt hollowed out.

"I am not sure I can feel those things anymore," she
admitted, voice trembling.

The serpent tilted its head.
"Perhaps."
Its voice lowered like a ritual chant.
"But you may feel them again. *Is that enough?*"

Eve's throat tightened.

She looked inward. Underneath her broken body.

Into the places where her spirit had splintered.
Into the bleeding ache that Adam had carved into her.
Into the shame, a foreign thing she had not known
existed until it wrapped around her like thorned vines.

But in that darkness, she found, a spark.

She thought of Lilith's garden.
The place of longing, and now of love.
The way the orchids had bloomed when she spoke
Lilith's name aloud.
The way Lilith's lips had shaped her name like it was
worthy of worship.

Lilith did not need Eve.

Lilith *chose* Eve.

And Eve, in the deepest part of her heart, still wanted
to choose her back.

Even now, covered in dirt and dried blood, bruised
and trembling, she felt the thrum of that love inside
her like a distant heartbeat calling her home.

She could turn toward death.
Disappear into the roots of the tree.
End the ache.

But then there would be no more Lilith.
No more laughter shared under fig trees.
No more love to uncover, to grow into, to name again
and again.

"*I want to live*," she said softly.

The serpent bowed its head in acceptance.

"A choice," it said, "worthy of the name you carry."

Eve stood on shaky legs.

The world tilted for a moment, not from weakness,
but from weight.
Knowledge made her body feel heavier, like she was
now carved from something denser than clay.

She looked down at herself.
Her bruises.
Her torn skin.
The dried blood on her thighs.
The dirt beneath her nails.

The marks he had left.

Shame swelled up, hot and suffocating, but she held it at arm's length.

She straightened.

One step.
Then another.
Her legs were unsteady, but her heart, her heart felt certain.

She was walking toward her future.

Toward *Hope*.

Hope was the strange new feeling she felt blooming in her wounds.

Hope, tender and trembling, yet persistent.

Hope that Lilith would still want her.
Hope that healing, though impossible to imagine, might be found in the arms of the first woman.

Toward Lilith.
Toward love.
Toward herself, and a life she had chosen.

CHAPTER

TWENTY-ONE

The path beneath Eve's feet was familiar now, a soft trail where fig leaves whispered secrets and the wind carried the faintest echo of Lilith's longing.

The trees bristled as she passed, not in greeting, but in warning.
A tension ran through Eden like a shiver.
Birds took flight in sudden bursts.
A doe bolted across her path, white tail flashing like a comet fleeing catastrophe.

Eve paused.

The Garden had never behaved this way.
Eden was harmony, breath and balance, song and stillness.
But now the air thickened.
The soil trembled beneath her toes.

Something was wrong. The sky was growing dark

though it was still day.

Lilith's garden was close, Eve could *feel* her, but so was something else.
Something she feared.

Behind her, came a voice that sent ice through her veins.

"Eve!"

She froze.

Her heartbeat stuttered and then hammered against her ribs.

Adam.

She turned slowly, bracing herself as if facing a predator.
Her spirit recoiled instinctively, even before her mind caught up.

He was already upon her.

Adam's hair hung wild around his face.
His chest heaved with frantic breaths.
His eyes, once always warm, always steady, were hollow now, drowning in guilt and something else she couldn't name.

Desperation maybe.

Eve took a single step backward, toward the path that led to Lilith. But before she could turn and run like she intended, Adam said the one thing that could stop her.

"God spoke to me!" Adam cried.

She hesitated. And Adam stepped closer, voice cracking.

"He knows. He knows everything."

Eve's breath hitched.
Shame slammed into her like a blow.

Everything.
God saw *everything*?

Her stomach tightened painfully.

Did he know what she let Adam do?

"He said you broke his command," Adam said. "You ate the fruit."

Eve staggered.
Her knees nearly buckled beneath her.

That moment, when she had bitten the fruit, had been a blur of agony and surrender.
A plea for ending.
A reaching for nothingness.

She had survived it.
But the truth was unchangeable.

She had broken God's one law.

Her throat closed.

Adam stepped forward, voice rising.

"And he cast us out! Out of paradise. He said this is your punishment. *Our* punishment, for what you made me do."

Eve's face crumpled.

"No," she whispered, shaking her head. "No, Adam. I didn't.."

"He cast us out!" Adam shouted over her.
"Both of us. The Garden is to be lost to us forever!"

The sky answered him.

A crack of thunder split the air overhead.
Lightning licked across the clouds like claws.
The wind twisted violently, ripping leaves from their branches.

Eve's heart and mind raced.
The path to Lilith, just ahead, still glowed with peaceful blue clear sky.
The scent of figs drifting like a promise.

Lilith was waiting.
Lilith was expecting her.
Lilith was her future.

The ground shook beneath them, a warning, or a boundary forming.

Eve turned to run. But Adam was faster.

Adam caught her arm.
His fingers dug painfully into her skin. Just as the light shifted and the world pulled back.

Eve screamed as the world tore itself open. And then, Darkness. Heat. Dust.

Eve hit the ground hard.

Adam fell beside her, coughing, choking on debris.

When Eve opened her eyes, the world was no longer
Eden.

No lush leaves.
No golden soil.
No familiar hum of creation.

And no Lilith.

Only dust.
Dry, cracked earth.
A burning sky.

The air scraped her throat like sandpaper.
Her skin prickled with heat.
The ground was sharp beneath her bare feet.

Eve whipped around.

The place where Lilith's path had been, where the air
once shimmered with life and longing, was only
barren stone now.

Adam rose slowly to his feet.
He looked around the barren wasteland with wide,
hollow eyes, a mixture of disbelief and relief twisting
his features. After a long moment, her turned to look
back at her.

"Looks like…" he murmured, "…it is only us once
again."

Eve stared at him. Her shoulders sagged. Tears spilled
down her cheeks. Then she looked back to the place
where the path to Lilith had just been.

She remembered being outside the garden with Lilith.
How grateful she had been that she did not belong to

this world. She remembered how Lilith had returned them home when it was too much. Eve closed her eyes hard and thought desperately of Eden. But she couldn't shake the feeling it would not work, that she no longer belonged there.

Because this was God's will. His punishment for what she had done. And she had gotten Adam cast out with her. As bad as he had done to her, surely this was worse.

They were alone. Again.

But this time, *it was all her fault*.

CHAPTER

TWENTY-TWO

The world outside Eden was not empty.

It was endless.

Mountains rose from the horizon like the shoulders of sleeping giants.
Rivers gnashed their way through stone, unruly and gray with silt.
The soil clung to their feet with the weight of mud but offered nothing willingly.
Fruit did not hang ready.
Leaves did not open themselves to gentle hands.

Nothing came freely.

Eve and Adam learned quickly; this world had to be worked, bled for, pleaded with, broken open just to survive.

They tore roots from the ground until their palms
blistered.
They coaxed fire from dry reeds.
They pressed mud and clay into walls that cracked
beneath the sun's glare.

Nights froze.
Days burned.

Lions did not lie beside lambs here.
Animals no longer spoke to Eve, or if they did, hunger
had twisted their voices into snarls she could not
understand.

Eden had been a cradle.
This world was a crucible.

Still, Eve stayed with Adam.

Not out of love.
Not out of fear.
But because she believed it was her penance.

She had eaten the fruit.
She had been cast out, Adam liked to remind her.
And she believed him. How else would he had known
about her eating from the tree, if not from God
himself.

She believed *everything* was her fault.

So, she bore the burden.
Guilt was heavy enough to shape a life.

They wandered for years.
Time, slippery and gentle in Eden, became harsh and
linear here.
The world moved on without waiting for them.

Eventually, they found people, just as Lilith had said, they were not all there was.

There were nomads, and villages, where they spoke of distant rising empires.

Eve watched them in awe.

Lilith had been right about everything.
Life existed outside the Garden.
It had always existed.

These people accepted Adam and Eve after long hesitation, after tests of strength and usefulness.
The villagers taught them how to hunt, how to cure hides, how to weave thick cloaks from wool.

Eve learned quickly.

Adam, too. Adam also told stories of Eden, God, and the Devil. Some doubted, some held his stories as gospel and sang them wherever they went. Eve refused to speak about their life before and lived a quiet life.

They built a home.

A small one, but a home, nonetheless.

Eve told herself she should be grateful.

In time, Eve bore children. One after another, the pain splitting her open like lightning through a tree.

It was agony. It reminded her of the pain the last time a man made use of her body. Was this pain the echo of that? Her screams tore through the huts like storm winds.

The burns of childbirth left her shaking for days.

But then, in her arms, a small man of her own making.

Soft lungs inhaling the world for the first time.
Tiny fingers curling around hers.
Eyes wide and dark, like little mirrors of the sky.

She named the first **Cain**.
The second, **Abel**.
Later came Seth, and others that reminded her of
Lilith naming things into being.

Eve loved her children fiercely.
But this love was different. This love was
complicated.
Every time she saw Adam's jawline in Seth, her chest
tightened.
Every time Abel smiled with Adam's smile, her breath
stuttered.
Every time Cain's temper flared in early childhood,
she felt a tremor of fear.

She withdrew without wanting to.
Touched them lightly, carefully, as though she feared
her own affection might scorch them.

She kept going.

Because that was life now.

Not paradise but endurance, with rare pockets of joy.

The women of the village became her solace. They

shared their griefs by the fireside, their laughter in the weaving huts, their secrets while bathing in the cold river.

And Eve listened.

Every story was the same.
Different in detail, identical in essence.

Men took.
Women endured.
Women bent so their sons could stand.

This dynamic wasn't all Earth's daughters had inherited from Eve.

Even if she could manage to forget the trauma, her body wouldn't. No woman's would.

It seemed all the women in the villages went through repeated cycles like the Moon above this world, they felt the echo of her pain.

When their bodies ached, and blood fell down their thighs, and they felt her anger or sorrow. Sometimes it could last days.

Beyond that, there was something else.

She saw it in their eyes. The flinch. The glance over the shoulder. The fear.

As if they all remembered something ancient and unfinished. A wound passed down like wisdom.

Was her assault at the hands of Adam the catalyst for this generational curse.

As their children grew and the village prospered,
Adam changed too.

He became quieter.
More resigned.

Though he had never again raised his hand in anger
toward her after Eden.

She could never forget. The only way she had been
able to fulfill her *wifely duties* was to let her mind
wander. Back through Eden. He had his way with her
body, because in those moments she would leave it.

Adam never questioned why she didn't move beneath
him anymore.

He didn't want the answer.

Sometimes, at night, when the village slept, Eve
would lie awake with her back to Adam.

The stars above this world were farther than the stars
of Eden.
Colder.
Older.

She would stare at them until tears slipped into her
hair.

And then the dreams would come.

Dreams of Lilith.

Her laughter in Eve's ear.

Her hands tracing the curve of her hip.
Her lips brushing her throat.
Her voice whispering Eve's name like a summoning
spell.

Shortly after Abel took his first steps and began
clinging to her side, Eve noticed Cain more closely.

The boy's jealousy burned like a coal.
His anger sparked too easily.
He shoved his siblings.
He scowled when others were praised.
He frightened the smaller children.

Eve saw Adam in him.

Not the Adam she first knew, gentle, content.

The Adam who struck her.
The Adam who forced her.
The Adam who insisted she was his, even when she
was breaking beneath him.

Fear bloomed inside her like a bruise that would never
heal.

She realized then,
Cain did not just inherit Adam's face.

She couldn't stay and watch any longer.

She could not breathe in this life.
Not with Adam.
Not with her memories.

Not with the fear that one day she might look at her son the same way she had come to see his father.

Eve remembered the serpent's question:

*"You may feel joy again.
Is that enough?"*

For the first time in years, Eve felt the answer inside her chest like a flame catching dry grass.

Yes. It was.

Eve rose before dawn.

The world outside the hut was black and silent.
Frost shimmered on the ground like shattered stars.

She wrapped herself in a cloak she had woven from sheep's wool.
She packed bread and dried beans and fruit into a small satchel.
She filled a waterskin.

She moved to the corner where her children slept, curled together in a nest of linen and fur.

She knelt beside them.
Touched each head softly.

"Seth," she whispered.
"Abel."
"Cain."

She kissed each brow.

She slipped out of the hut with silent steps.

The air was bitter.
The sky empty.

The world stretched endless before her.

But she walked.

She walked with purpose this time.
Not wandering.
Not exiled.
Choosing.

She did not know the way.
But she knew the direction.

East of the rising sun.
Toward the place where her heart had once
blossomed.
Toward the place where orchids bloomed at her feet.

Toward Eden.

Though Eden was closed to her, she would find where
it once stood.
If Lilith loved her still, and Eve believed she did,
maybe she would find her.

And if it took the rest of her life,
she would walk
until her path
found its way
back to love.

CHAPTER

TWENTY-THREE

Years stretched on like long shadows since Eden. And more still since Eve first turned her gaze back toward it.

She wandered now among the descendants of wanderers, nomads who traced forgotten rivers, moved with seasons, and spoke in stories shaped by hunger and dust. They welcomed her, this quiet stranger with eyes that held dawn and ruin. They did not ask her origins. In this wilderness, everyone carried secrets. They only sought the refuge of numbers, the warmth of shared labor, and the faint illusion of safety.

But they were all seeking something that kept them from holding still.

Eve traveled with them, helping gather reeds, grinding grains between stones, weaving blankets from wool and flax. At night they huddled around a fire that hissed and spat at the wind, drawing women and children close while men patrolled the edges of camp with spears carved from bone.

This night, the flames licked high, bright enough to mimic a dying sun, and Eve sat at its fringe, arms wrapped around her knees, her eyes reflecting every flicker like they were searching for someone inside it.

The women shared tales to soothe the children or frighten them into caution, warnings wrapped as lullabies. An older woman, with hair like braided silver and hands cracked from decades of sun, carried on with one sung tale.

Her voice rose soft at first, then strong.

"And so the Demoness prowls in the night,
with wings like shadow and a voice like silk.
She slips through tents, whispers lies into men's ears,
seduces them from their beds,
and drains them of their souls."

The children gasped. A few hid behind their mothers' shoulders.

The storyteller leaned closer to the fire, its glow painting her wrinkles in gold.

"Some say she steals newborns," the woman went on. "Hates mothers. That's why we leave salt by our windows, to keep her out. They say.."

"What's her name?" a child asked, fearful, thumb hovering at her lips.

"**Lilith**." The woman spat the name like a thorn. "Once a creature of great wisdom and beauty. But she thought herself better than man, better than God. So she rebelled against him, and became the Devil." she lifted a bony finger "That, is what happens when a woman forgets her place."

Children drew closer to their mothers.
Some women nodded with resigned understanding.
Others pressed their lips tight, as if the words scraped something raw inside them.

And Eve, Eve rose.

Unable to stay seated or silent any longer.
Her body moved before thought.
Moved with something older than these stories, older than her shame, older than Adam's corrupted legend.

The women took notice as she stepped forward.
Her presence was not loud, but it was absolute.
A hush descended so deep that even the flames seemed to lean toward her.

Eve's voice came low, but it carried like truth itself.

"That is not the true story."

The storyteller blinked up at her.
The children watched her with wide eyes.
Women straightened and looked between each other.

Eve stepped closer to the fire, letting its warmth kiss her skin.
Shadows danced over her face, making her look both young and immeasurably ancient.

"Lilith was not cursed," Eve said, voice even as hammered stone.
"She chose freedom over blind obedience."

A few women exchanged glances, some hopeful, some wary.

"She would not kneel to a man who saw her as lesser. And when she left, he feared her power. So, he named her monster. Thief. Whore. Devil."

Her gaze swept the circle.

"It was easier than admitting she was simply beyond his control."

A ripple, shame, recognition, anger, passed through the women.

The storyteller sputtered, "But the songs say.."

"*I was there.*"

The crackle of burning wood filled the stunned silence.

Eve's voice did not shake.
Her shoulders were straight, her spine unbent.
She stood in the firelight like a pillar carved before time.

"There were no children to steal. No wings. And certainly, no hunger for men."
Eve almost smiled at the absurdity of it.

"Her voice was like silk, yes. But not to lure men. It was to teach, to guide. To love." Eve shared the truth she had long neglected. "She *loved me*. Not to ruin me, but to awaken me. And when I gave up on myself, on her. The world rewrote her story. *But I remember*."

She pressed a hand to her chest.

The women and children all stared in rapture, trying to figure out if Eve spoke truth.

"You were taught to fear her." Eve said, gently now, turning to the woman who had been telling the tale. "But tell me. How many times have you been told to make yourself quiet, small, obedient? How many times have you swallowed your fire to make yourself safe?"

Eve looked into the fire so they could all see her face.

Women looked down, looked away.

"Mothers," Eve said, voice aching, "how many times have you warned your daughters that men frighten easily, and that frightened animals grow violent?"

Now, eyes glistened in the firelight.

"That submission," Eve said, "is not your nature. It is the cage Lilith tried to break. To free me from and show me what I deserve."

The child who had asked Lilith's name earlier tugged at Eve's skirt.

"Did it work?" she whispered.

Eve considered the question carefully.

She thought of the way Lilith empowered her, of what she deserved, and where she belonged.

Her eyes glistened.

"Yes," she answered, voice thick with emotion. "I think it has."

"I am no longer ashamed of what was done to me. Only that I let myself believe I was less deserving because of it. Less deserving of Lilith's love, or my place in Eden."

As Eve took a deep breath, a wind rose. It swept across the valley, and Eve instantly recognized the scent that rode on that wind.

Sweet figs.

She closed her eyes and inhaled, all the way down to the place she had once starved of joy.
Her lungs filled with memory.
With longing.

When she opened her eyes, she was no longer among the caravan.

The fire was gone.
The valley was gone.
The cold wind was gone.

Eve found herself in Lilith's garden once more. A place she thought she would only ever see in her dreams.

Eve had returned.

Where she belonged.

Back at the caravan she had left behind, for the first time in generations, no one put salt at their windows that night.

EPILOGUE

Eve stepped forward into the whole of Eden, but it was not Eden.

Not the Eden she had known at least.

Eden no longer breathed the way she remembered.

The air felt strained, not barren, but unsettled. Vines coiled too tightly around trunks. Blossoms bloomed and fell in the same hour. The river ran faster than it once had, biting and breaking away its banks as if trying to outrun itself.

Nothing had withered.

But nothing was fully at peace.

"Lilith?" Eve called.

Her voice vanished into the overgrown canopy.

No answer came.

She searched the grove where they had once knelt in tall grass. The bank where the salmon had fought their way upstream. The shaded bend of river where Lilith had first taught her how to guide a vine without breaking it.

Every place held her absence like a bruise.

The serpent waited in the branches of the once forbidden tree.

"You return," it hissed out.

Eve's breath was already unsteady. "Where is she?"

The serpent regarded her with its ancient, unblinking gaze.

"When you didn't come back, she searched."

"For me?" Eve whispered.

"For you."

Eve's knees nearly gave way.

"She walked every path. Every clearing. She called your name until even the birds grew silent. She questioned the heavens. She questioned me."

The serpent's coils shifted along the branch.

"She was forced to ask the question she feared most."

Eve swallowed. "What question?"

"Why you did not return."

The air seemed to tighten. The serpent's tongue flicked once.

"She learned what he did to you."

The world stilled.

No breeze. No birdsong.

Even the river seemed to hesitate.

Eve closed her eyes.

"She did not rage at first," the serpent continued. "She grew quiet."

The ground beneath Eve's feet trembled faintly, as if remembering.

"She knelt where you once stood. She pressed her hand into the soil and asked if it had felt your fear."

Eve's chest fractured.

"And when she understood that Eden had witnessed it and remained unchanged—"

The serpent's voice lowered.

"She did not."

A wind tore through the grove without warning.

Leaves ripped from branches. Fruit split and fell before ripeness. The river surged over its banks as if something vast had entered it.

"She did not scream," the serpent said. "She did not weep. She rose."

Eve felt the violence in the air as if it were happening again — as if the trees still remembered the force of it.

"She cursed nothing," the serpent went on. "She named nothing. She simply refused."

The vines tightened around their trunks. The grass bent flat under invisible pressure.

Eve's breath came shallow.

"I—"

"She did not condemn you."

The serpent's gaze did not soften.

The wind faltered.

The violence in the trees subsided, not from peace, but from decision.

"But she could not contain the fury or the grief," the serpent said, "It changed her."

Eve stared at the shifting landscape around her, at blossoms that bloomed too quickly, at roots splitting earth as if trying to escape it.

"I didn't mean to..." Eve started to explain

"You did nothing. When she learned what had been *done to you*. She was only more desperate to find you."

Eve was overcome with relief that Lilith didn't blame her.

"Then she learned you ate from the Tree…" the serpent continued " and she would hear no more.

Her rage and grief burst forth, devouring every corner

of the garden in longing. One that wouldn't be satiated

"She did this?" Eve whispered.

"She is bound to it," the serpent replied. "As you are."

Eve sank to her knees beneath the forbidden tree.

The fruit above her hung heavy and indifferent.

"Though she no longer felt that bond," the serpent said, not unkindly. "She no longer felt she belonged to the garden, she only belonged to her rage."

The wind beyond the trees howled, distant, relentless.

"She will not be gentle with that world," the serpent added.

A tremor of something like awe passed through Eve's grief.

"What do you mean?" Eve asked.

"Lilith abandoned the garden that flourished with memories of love lost, She now roams Earth seeking to end her longing once again."

Eve was shocked and devastated.

"She seeks another to end her longing?" Eve asked, wanting it to be true as much as she didn't.

"Yesss," the serpent hissed, "another named vengeance."

Eve pressed her palms into the soil.

"Will she return," Eve said faintly.

The serpent did not answer.

The silence was answer enough.

Eve lifted her face toward the sky, still endless, still blue.

"I will wait," she said.

"As long as it takes."

THE END

(For Now)

Thank you for reading

More from A.M. Glory soon